Superhuman Tales

Superhuman Tales

by
Victor-Emile Michelet

Translated, annotated and introduced by
Brian Stableford

A Black Coat Press Book

ISBN 978-1-61227-795-0. First Printing. September 2018. Published by Black Coat Press, an imprint of Hollywood Comics.com, LLC, P.O. Box 17270, Encino, CA 91416. All rights reserved. Except for review purposes, no part of this book may be reproduced or transmitted in any form or by any means, electronic or mechanical, including photocopying, recording, or by any information storage and retrieval system, without permission in writing from the publisher. The stories and characters depicted in this novel are entirely fictional. Printed in the United States of America.

TABLE OF CONTENTS

Introduction

All but one of the stories in this collection are taken from *Contes surhumains* by Victor-Émile Michelet, which was originally published by Chamuel in 1900; a new edition was issued in 1907 by the Bibliothèque Générale d'Édition. The other story, *Holwennioul*, was published in 1899 in the periodical *L'Humanité Nouvelle*, of which the author was one of the editors, before the relevant pages were extracted and issued independently as a booklet, having presumably been written after the collection went to press, although it appeared in advance of it. Some of the other stories in the collection had also previously appeared in periodicals with which the author was intimately associated. "La Redémptrice" (tr. as "The Redemptrix") and "Incantation par les dix noms divins" (tr. as "Incantation by the Ten Divine Names") both appeared initially in his *Psyché*, the former as a serial in 1891-92 and the latter in a single issue in 1892; in general, the stories reflect the first and most experimental phase of the author's career, developed during the gilded era of the *fin-de-siècle*.

Victor-Émile Michelet (1861-1938)—who was not related to the famous historian Jules Michelet—was involved in the French Occult Revival from his early youth, when he was a close friend of Stanislas de Guaita; he later collaborated with Guaita, "Papus" (Gérard Encausse) and Joséphin Péladan in the reformulation of the eighteenth-century Martinist Order, originally founded by Martinez de Pasqually and provided with much of its occult philosophy by Louis-Claude Saint-Martin. Michelet was also a fervent admirer of Édouard Schuré, another leading figure of the nineteenth century revival, who wrote numerous works of fiction inspired by his occult researches.

It was by no means uncommon for lifestyle fantasists who represented themselves as mystics and magicians also to be poets, like Guaita, or writers of imaginative prose fiction, like Schuré and the prolific Péladan. The similarly-prolific Jules Bois also wrote several novels in which he imported occult ideas into quasi-naturalistic fictions, following in the footsteps of Louis Jacolliot. Papus recruited the accomplished feuilletonist Jules Lermina—whose eldest daughter was married to a specialist occult bookseller and publisher—to develop his story ideas into publishable works. The great pioneer of the Occult Revival, Éliphas Lévi (Alphonse-Louis Constant) had also dabbled in literary fantasy before becoming a wholehearted lifestyle fantasist.

The overlap in question worked both ways; many writers of the *fin-de-siècle* were drawn to take an interest in fashionable occultism, especially those of the Symbolist school, who found a perfectly natural affinity between their literary method and the elaborate symbolism of occultism, and while some interested writers, like Joris-Karl Huysmans, retained a careful skeptical distance, others developed a degree of commitment. For some, like Gabriel de Lautrec and Frédéric Boutet, that commitment was a temporary flirtation, while for others, such as Jean Rameau and Maurice Magre, it became a lifelong obsession. Of all the writers in question, Victor-Émile Michelet was the one who had his feet most firmly planted in both camps, cultivating a considerable reputation as a poet while committing himself wholeheartedly to the lifestyle fantasy of an initiate.

Michelet's prose fiction is relatively sparse, comprising a thin oeuvre by comparison with his numerous poetry collections, most notably *La Porte d'Or* [The Golden Gate] (1902), *L'Espoir merveilleux* [The Marvelous Hope] (1908) and *La Descente de Vénus aux enfers* [The Decent of Venus into Hell] (1931), several plays—mostly unproduced—and a number of essays in mysticism, most famously *Le Secret de la Chevalerie* [The Secret of Chivalry] (1930). He was also a literary critic of some significance, the longest of his essays being a critical study of *Villiers de l'Isle-Adam* (1910), whose influence on his own prose is considerable, particularly evident in *Holwennioul*, which clearly takes a good deal of inspiration from Villiers' flamboyant *Akedysseril* (1886). With only a few exceptions, Michelet's publications in volume form were a trifle belated, his career only taking off when he was in his forties, although he had long been an enthusiastic participant in the thriving culture of literary cafés and salons, as well as the parallel occult circles. Although his presidency of the Societé des Poètes Français in 1910 only followed the publication of his first collection by eight years, he must have seemed by then to his electors to be a representative of the older generation.

The wide circle of Michelet's literary acquaintances is reflected in the dedications that he frequently attached to his poems and stories, and he also had no hesitation in declaring his key influences; *Contes surhumains* features a florid prefatory dedication in Latin to "Ludovicus-Claudius Saint-Martin, Edgardus Poe, Gerardus de Nerval, Carolus Baudelaire, Eliphas Levi, Augustus Villiers de l'Isle-Adam and P. F. G. Lacuria."[1] This does not mean, however, that his work is derivative; indeed, it is highly distinctive, to the extent that there is nothing else quite like it. Although it includes such modest qua-si-anecdotal pieces as "Entre tous les regards" (tr. as "Among all Gazes"), "Magie d'Amour" (tr. as "Amo-rous Magic"), "La Mort des amants" (tr. as "the Death of Lovers"), and an account of a clichéd posthumous appa-rition, "L'Inquiétante rose" (tr. as "The Disquieting Rose"), even those stories reveal a consistent ambition to push their various envelopes, which gives them a partic-ular edge. When, on the other hand, he strikes out into determined originality, as in his elaborate study of deca-dent ennui "Sardanapale" (tr. as "Sardanapalus") or his most famous story, "La Rédemptrice" (tr. as "The Redemptrix"), which offers an oblique view of a female Messiah, he does so with a determined verve.

Although the narrative formats of such fantasies as "L'Île de Joie" (tr. as "The Isle of Joy") and "Le Mystère d'une incarnation" (tr. as "The Mystery of an Incarna-tion") are stubbornly stereotypical, the author makes considerable efforts in those cases and others to distance his endeavors decisively from the conventional deploy-ments of the formulae. The latter story, in particular, draws both energy and charm from the earnest esoteri-cism of its central motif, and it exploits more poignantly than any of his other stories the curious idiosyncrasy of the author's perennial fascination with death. The former

---

[1] All these names were and remain famous except the last, Paul-François-Gaspard Lacuria (1806-1890), who wrote ex-tensively about the mystery of numbers—one of Michelet's favorite themes—and also published a slim collection of *Contes* (1885).

makes more orthodox use of the ironic spirit of the *conte cruel*, which dominated upmarket short fiction during the *fin-de-siècle*, but applies it to a graphic visionary fantasy with the peculiar obliquity that is almost a hallmark of the author's work.

It is that oblique rhetorical stance, above all, that recommends Michelet for serious consideration as a contributor to the tradition of French fantasy fiction, and isolates him from those Symbolists for whom symbolism was primarily a method, or even an affectation, and who applied it more straightforwardly. As befits an earnest lifestyle fantasist, Michelet took his fantasy and its symbolism very seriously, especially when its extrapolation led by convoluted paths to strange conclusions. As with many works of a similar stripe, his collection is more than the sum of its parts, and its totality is further enhanced by the supplementation of *Holwennioul*, which can be seen as a kind of summation of the author's adventures in prose fiction, and of his convictions in the field of mystical philosophy.

This translation was made from the version of the 1907 edition reproduced on the Bibliothèque Nationale's *gallica* website.

Brian Stableford

AMOUR IN ERROR

To Paul Bourget

My dear, my adorable, my beloved Lena, your heart absolves all weakness. You will forgive me, you have already forgiven me, if, at the present moment, I entertain a thought other than that of our amour and our death. What am I saying? You approve of my writing these pages; for it is necessary that they are written. Perhaps they will also have the virtue of bringing lovers back to a path to salvation from which the two of us were expelled, both victims of an initial error.

Lena, you will read these pages. They will not be any revelation to you. For between us there is no secret; but anxious silences flow between our souls like dead rivers. Certainly, in order for us to understand one another, words are as unnecessary as the adornment of roses in your ash-blonde hair. How we have suffered, though, from those silences, intercepting the intercourse of our thoughts.

We always lived, Lena and I, occupied with one another. If the years have separated our bodies, our twin spirits were indissolubly linked from the cradle to the grave. Lena, you were engendered for me by a kiss of the dolor of joy. Our first gazes caressed one another. Lena did not know either a mother or a father, and like her, I was born an orphan, but few of the living could have a childhood as happy.

Our first eighteen years went by in peace and felicity. May the earth be light upon the gentle old man who welcomed us in order to raise us thus. Lena and I grew up side by side with that excellent man, Envel, and his old maidservant Michelle. How did that solitary philosopher come to assume responsibility for our two childhoods? He maintained a silence on that matter that we never sought to unravel. What did our origins matter to us? His heart had every tenderness, and his intelligence every strength. He had penetrated the most mysterious arcana of life. In company with him and the good Michelle, our candid eyes did not know tears.

We lived thus for eighteen years without quitting our beautiful green valley, our land of joy. Our house overlooked the little river snaking through the meadows toward the nearly sea. Bushy forests crowned the circular horizons of the hills, and the wind from the land and the wind from the sea, on brushing the crowns of the beeches and the pines, renounced their violence in order to descend in musical mildness into our valley. The refuge had been chosen in order that nature would neglect to wound us.

Except for three months of winter, we lived on an undulating green and gold carpet. Compact florescences succeeded one another around us: flowers everywhere, yellow, violet and red. Our eyes opened to their beauty. Perhaps the constant reflection of those solar flowers is still perpetuated in Lena's topaz eyes. The earth offered us from the outset what it created of the most charming and most innocent. Insensate, later we demanded anguish from it. It never refuses.

Our twin souls grew there in plenitude. I do not remember that any desire ever sprang to Lena's mind without an identical desire springing forth in mine. Our placid dreams soared in parallel. We had no suspicion of any disharmony between us, or in the world. And when, in the evening, after a pleasant day playing in the meadows, Envel's white beard leaned over our foreheads, the old man's tender smile dismissed from our breasts the malefices of the night.

His voice, so limpidly sonorous that his hand doubtless never had the power to wound, revealed to us the allegory of life. He talked to us about nature and the gods, rarely about human beings. He did not judge it appropriate to preoccupy us with their history, the annals of their desires, their sufferings, their struggles and their crimes. But his speech informed us of the essential reality, evoked for us the spirits of things whose beauty our faithful eyes penetrated. And our dear valley opened the perspective of its spiritual planes to us. Behind the bark of oak trees we knew the green hamadryads. Beneath the earth that our joyful feet trod, we divined the incessant labor of gnomes. When in our river, Lena and I swam in convoy, we perceived subtle water spirits, eternally young naiads, gliding over our naked and chaste flesh as well as frightened trout. And the soul of gilded flowers did not quiver in the silence of the evenings without ours communicating with it. The spirits of things, the secondary divinities of our bodies, were as familiar to us as our dogs.

Beyond our horizons, further away than our flowery meadows and our forests of maples and aspens, did another world exist? No curiosity accompanied our suppositions; no desire tempted us to know cities, to see the agitation of the human crowd. Sometimes, we went down the low and salty river as far as the sea, from which we did not return any more emotional.

Thus adolescence covered us with its bright wings. Our hearts became graver and our laughter more explosive. We sensed the beauty blossoming around us as in the irises of our valleys, and amour enveloping us like the perpetual air.

When Lena's dear, sweet head was weary, and weighed upon my shoulder, the rose of her thought, always as sumptuous as the brightness of roses in the dawn, I contemplated it without a thought, without desire and without a dream—oh, with no suspicion that I would one day suffer worse than atrocious wounds from those candid young eyes, also inhabited by an equal dolor. The pearly oval of her face was lightly carmined beneath my lips.

Our pure caresses were still ignorant of sensual disturbances. Our twin hearts beat in accordance with such a eurhythmia of amour that the effluvia of our nubile flesh were enfevered by our blood. Yes, happiness could have accompanied us to the tomb. Our amour might have had the sweetness of incest. One day, our embrace might have been excited in accordance with the desire of the earth. And perhaps we might have died of it, for the angels of the moon come in search of couple of souls that fuse entirely into a single androgynous soul in an ecstasy as divine as ours would have been.

One evening however, Envel pronounced mysterious words. He kissed us even more tenderly than usual, and the next day, he did not wake up again. We shed our first tears. Old Michelle did not take long to follow her master into the flowery cemetery. The only beings who loved us were effaced from our horizon. Our amour remained a solitary flower. And although Envel had accustomed us to considering death as a simple modification of life, a sadness insinuated itself into our ingenuousness.

Let us not accuse either destiny or human beings; peril or misfortune, alas, come from ourselves.

The evening when we found the old vagabond unconscious in the forest, the world was revealed to us under a new aspect. The decrepit old man had collapsed, of lassitude, poverty and despair. We carried him to our house, and for a fortnight, our youth watched over his debility. He related to us, in his simple and coarse speech, his life of suffering. Then, one day, he picked up his staff and went away—toward what roads? But Lena's bright eyes remained more pensive beneath my less certain lips.

Yes, our juvenile felicity no longer blossomed like the candor of roses. The dolor of the world had crossed the circle of our horizons in order to force the virginity of our joy. No sentiment penetrated Lena's bosom without invading mine, for we had the same soul in two forms. A shadow grew between our kisses, arrived from beyond our atmosphere; a shadow weighed upon the spontaneity of our dreams.

Lena's dear blonde head learned over my breast, and her adored mouth expressed our common thought:

"My love, we will go toward people. The imperious voice of the suffering is calling to us. It is singing an incantation deleterious to our solitary happiness, and our ears have received it like a poisoned arrow. The distress of the world is crying for help to us, rich in youth, beauty and amour."

And we marched, in enthusiasm and torment, toward the human world.

I shall always, always remember that summer morning, that somber summer morning when we crossed the threshold of a city for the first time. On the edge of the city, a wide river ran. The river was flowing toward the unknown sea, and we were going toward imminent anguish. In a dirty gray sky the nascent sunlight descended over the slow waters. Bleak fishermen abandoned themselves in dilapidated boats. We traversed the bridge by which people arrived in order to disperse within the sickly walls. Along the water's edge the sad houses of prostitutes were strung out; and on the road, formless caryatids were walking, peasants carrying heavy baskets on their heads.

She also passed, the beautiful young woman with whom you will sleep tomorrow, insouciant young man that I envy, my fellow and yet so different! Men filed past, bent over, carters leading poor weary horses. Emaciated dogs were pulling heavy carriages, and twisted beggars were limping toward the streets. All those bodies were dolorous, deformed by painful and sterile life. All those faces were sculpted by suffering. The city seemed to us to be plaintive and accursed. Lena, it was the city where our hearts were lacerated for the first time.

Despair clutched our bosoms. We hugged one another, oppressed and faint. With her lips raised toward mine, Lena repeated: "We are rich in youth, beauty and amour."

Years have passed, seven sinister years of separation; oh, we know them now, seven years of death. We have found one another across the world. We have returned to our valley. And here we both are, still young, bewildered in our wounded amour, and using our hearts in vain to wash away our memories.

On the day when we separated, the earth stole away beneath our bodies, stirred by our last kiss. But the image of a fallacious duty demanded that separation of our novice minds. Oh, the true duty was to create in the world the virtue of a magnificent and solitary amour. But the enthusiasm of sacrifice, the folly of renunciation, filled our breasts. Insidious fate triumphed.

What did I do during those seven accursed years? I attempted to act in accordance with noble and pure thoughts. Like all men, I showed weaknesses. My arm did not realize the ambition of my desire, and the glory of my thought weakened under my embraces. But I can swear on the tender forehead of Lena that no aspiration other than that of righteousness guided my footsteps. I marched toward human misery with the determination to soothe it or die trying.

No, I was not born for that effort. I lacked the violent faith it requires. I employed my strength in accordance with my power. I have served harmony, peace and justice. But the ignominy of the oppressors, the cowardice of the oppressed and the weakness of all induced the sense of revolt in me, and I evoked wrath as a generous law. I uttered clamors, the echo of which still envelops my name, a name that was, for a few simply hearts, a flame of hope. Oh, how disappointed they were! Like all those who hope, alas! My ill-born effort only engendered disasters, only struck the black pole of its luminous goal. Had I not dreamed of passing through the crowd as a sower of amour with full hands? I unmuzzled more hatred. Woe betide the abortive work of the impotent passer-by!

How many times, a discouraged fighter, I allowed my forehead to fall into my weary hands! But Lena's last words lived in my bosom: "We are rich in youth, beauty and amour." I raised my head again. Anguish, however, did not quit my shadow, and with it, agonized by absence, the image of my beloved Lena.

On one evening of defeat—I had gone to fight for a courageous small population defending their liberty and their lives—I remained on the battlefield, wounded. Under the glacial light of the stars, the gentle hands of a woman were imposed on my feverish brow. In the exaltation of the moment, my lips murmured a name, always the same: *Lena.*

It was her. Having learned that I was part of that army, she had come as a nurse and found me on the bloody earth. And we came back to the valley of our childhood, swearing never to quit it henceforth—oh, never again!

Yes, the refuge of our childhood has received our troubled youth benignly. Amid the gilded flowers, the smiling phantoms of our adolescent joys still float. The soul of our kisses of old palpitates around the branches, and the voice of the breeze in the pines sings the hymn of our revolved emotions. Our amour has gown like the trees. Life, so hard for human beings, offers truces to ecstatic lovers.

Alas, Lena, cruel shadows pass between your loyal beauty and the flame of my amour. What a diadem of anguish for your pale gold tresses! And over your perfumed breasts my lips have only tasted a savor of joy. Has the solemn night when our amour was exalted triumphed over our torments? Why can we not give it that power? Lena, I have entered into your embrace a virgin.

No other woman has troubled my breast with desire. The man haunted by a unique amour is magnetized by a radiant prestige to which the tenebrous hearts of women run for enlightenment. How many have come to brush my trace with their warm shadow. They have passed on, vain temptresses.

Now, during the seven years of absence, my beloved, what was your destiny? Of the slightest event that has creased your brow, nothing is hidden from me, nor any of your dreams. Our past hours appeared to us as transparent as crystal. In any case, even if I were unaware of the vanished events, could you suffer from them any less, my poor, poor plaintive darling?

On different planes, my adventure was yours. Yes, like my just determination, in which my militant energy became harmful, so your beauty and tenderness engendered misfortune. And it is of that that we still think, in which we languish without respite, and the dead flower of memory exhales its poisonous breath perpetually. Lena, when your beauty leaned over the suffering of men, it wounded souls. Toward it, men have cried out desperately in amour; and you have given yourself to them as you would have given all your blood...

I know that your amour has always been consecrated to me without division. I know your tears, your despairs. Oh, I know them all too well! And the worry no longer quits your breast, and the obsession of things of old gnaws us and lacerates us. Oh, the circles of shadow around your excessively bright eyes, and the pallor of your dear lips!

Yes, the past is never anything but an image attached to our personal atmosphere, a living image nourished by our essential substance. Can we not destroy it? Can we not kill, like a malevolent beast, the obsessive creation that our own weakness maintains in existence? Does the hand not have the power to efface an image inscribed in the light, where my anxious eyes are exasperated by its contemplation? The river Lethe, the lustral water of forgetfulness, only flows for the dead. But no soul attains it, none plunges into it in order to dissolve the obsessions riveted to the shoulders, without having been led there by a powerful and intact will. Juno alone has the privilege of bathing her beautiful loins every year in the spring of Kanathos, in order to emerge from it virgin in body and soul. Our will, enchained by passion, has lost that proud liberty of its gesture, which would sweep from our horizon the hallucinating specter of past events.

Oh, voracious specters, vampiric memories whose mouths delve into our amour to extract the joy therefrom, we bear our grim weight in our loins. What can deliver us? What can render us serenity, the pacific strength of initial amour?

What? Death, perhaps.

O Death, liberatrix with pale fingers, refuge of those to whom life was error and torment, yes, like so many others we have evoked your footsteps of the supreme visitor, So many lovers before us have forced your coming, by iron and fire, by water and poison. Were they so demented, to flee the soft light, so dense with cruelty around them? No couple in love have ever thrown themselves into the arms of death in order to seek annihilation there. All of them wanted to seize the hope of a definitive and perfect union. O Death, they desired your night as the most beautiful of nights of amour. They have not implored the destruction of life but its multiplication under your law. For the sure instinct of wounded hearts to love lifts the veil of the most mysterious arcana.

To die? So often, after the ephemeral enthusiasm of sacred sensuality—impotent, alas to deliver our sad amour from its torment—so often, in her pale face, Lena's gilded eyes, circled more by anguish than delight, implored me toward the threshold of the tomb! There, the weight attaching us to woe—the delightful and fatal weight of your body, your too-beloved body that was in the arms of men—would dissolve, and, free and light, our amour would pursue its redeemed flight in the purity of shades.

Then the grave image of Envel surged forth on the edge of our exitial dream. Envel? He knew distant secrets, heavy for humans but of which his white head bore the burden smiling. From the cycles that it had crossed, his shade was able to approach our dear foreheads without difficulty. And we summoned that dear memory to our aid meekly. Yes, his thought descended into us like a friendly river.

"Those who give themselves to death," he affirmed, "provoke upon their heads a reaction proportionate to their attempt. The violated norm takes possession of its violator all the more strongly. The state of your being that you renounce will seize you again with a grip of iron, vain refractory prey. By means of your leap outside the earth, you would not elude your suffering, a proof and conscience of your life. It would surround you with invincible arms. Would your will be able to escape them? Since it had already been vanquished by your despair, could it have the strength to triumph over your despair, corroborated by your flight into irreversibility?

"Your voluntary death would be a pact of alliance with fatality. You would not break its consequences. Can anyone who races to slavery attain liberty? The demi-lucid instinct of lovers informs them that death is the multiplier of life—yes, but life as they quit it. Stifled by passion, their inert will cannot attenuate, beyond the tomb, the rigor of the destiny by which it is evoked. On the plane corresponding to the vital hope, a fatal hand of darkness would present to them, more bitter still, the cup of anguish that their weak hands had rejected."

That revelation penetrated us, breathless and pensive. Then the soundless voice, the dear once-familiar voice that senses more subtle than our hearing perceived, continued, more tenderly:

"Children, chosen children, your path, traced by my hope, has slipped away from your footsteps. In order to seduce you into error, the insidious serpent that prowls around fortunate lovers has put on the noblest form. Its powerful attraction absorbs your essential impetus. Children, if it had been able to resist the vertigo of the fall, your amour would have given birth for the world the virtue of a Sign. The beauty of that solitary amour would have spread its perfume into the dolor of the world. All beauty is creative of joy. Two beings loving one another sublimely from the cradle to the grave, in the profundity of an unknown valley, bring, more than illusory sacrifices, a beneficial radiation into universal life. Children, poor children, I might have spoken too late, But if I had spoken sooner, you could not have understood."

Alas, yes, we have understood too late. Dear dolorous eyes of my Lena, will you see a pure horizon of joy one day?

May clement amour forgive us and aid us!

THE ISLE OF JOY

To Catulle Mendès

*If you pluck the flower of our hope from the earth,
it will be poisonous and mortal to you.*

The air was as sweet as a nascent amour in that first May dawn, and the Moon was entering into its third house. The young man had been marching toward the Occident for hours. He was perhaps twenty years old, and no one knew the things of ancient times better than him. Drops of dew constellated his blond hair. He traversed profound green valleys in which violet irises flowered in the shade of oak trees and rocky hills where gorse scratched his dogskin trousers. His footfalls frightened snakes as blue as his eyes shook spider-webs weighed down by adamantine dewdrops between the spiny tips of stems.

He arrived at the foot of a steep and very high rock, the flanks of which extended a few thin fir trees to the wrath of the west wind. The young man's heart beat more forcefully in his bosom. He scaled the rock. At the summit, he stopped. That summit formed a plateau overhanging a landscape whose circular horizon limited a distant sky. The young man looked northwards. The aspect of things did not respond to the appeal of his eyes, which studied space for a long time. Finally, toward the east, they projected a radiance of joy, and his arms instinctively launched toward the mirage of a desire, folded over his breast, while the sight engendered ecstasy.

Immemorial words, in the heart of the country, recounted the vision that enchanted the young traveler then. They evoked the enigmatic existence of a lake whose waters could only be perceived from the summit of a rock. On one single day of the year, every spring, a conjunction of stars, by virtue of the projection of a mysterious gleam, permitted the sight of a landscape that was ordinarily invisible. And strange rumors circulated regarding the apparition of that lake.

The old women of the region, while wearing out their distaffs during long winter evenings, divulged to children the magic of the uncertain sheet of water, which they or forgotten ancestors had seen. Many eyes had marveled at that dream. The most certain thing was that no bird had ever flown over that lake. When the wagtails migrated in flocks, they made a long detour to in order to avoid its vicinity. In the middle of the lake, always shrouded in violet-tinted mist, one discovered with great difficulty a confused mass, perhaps an island. Sometimes, the breeze that blew from the mountain opposite brought over the calm water delightful songs flown from the isle. And for having heard the murmurs of that music scattered in the night, the young shepherds of the surrounding area had remained pale and taciturn for a long time. But never had any man's boat opened the surface of those waters and found that fallacious island, where only creatures from other worlds could live.

And it was the heart of those mysterious waters, which the young matinal traveler discovered beneath the distant mists, that an obscure mass was veiled. Certainly, the waves, daughters of the attractive moon, had always enveloped the vacillating desires of souls with their vertigo. Beyond those waves, did a fatherland exist in which our intimate hopes were incarnated in glorious forms, in order to excite us with their embraces? There are Lethean waters that wash the past of all its pollutions and its pains, and Hippocrene waters that pour enthusiasm and strength into bosoms. The prince of the water sprites offers humans a mysterious pact. The breath of those waters infused with anguish the young man who had previously assailed perils and seductions without any disturbance. He closed his eyes, in order no longer to see except with his soul, and to collect himself in order to invoke, as in the most solemn hours of life, the smiling influences of his destiny.

A few moments later, the solitary traveler was walking in a subterranean tunnel. From a previous hour he retained the confused memory of a dream: a turning stone, a dagger-thrust in the breast of a scaly beast, the guardian of the threshold, and then a hectic descent into darkness. He walked, stumbling over animals of the darkness and the earth. Icy gusts devoured the sweat of his limbs. A voice that seemed to come from the heart of the earth said: "The gnomes are dominant, but the egregores of respiration are still less redoubtable than your own desire."[2]

How long did that groping march last? The young man never knew. But he inhaled deliverance by the first

---

[2] The term "égrégore" [egregore], derived from a gnomic reference in *Genesis*, was redefined and repopularized in the *fin-de-siècle* as a label for a kind of psychic vampire, moist memorably in a story by Jean Lorrain, "L'Égrégore" (1888; tr. as "The Egregore")

light of dawn. The majestic waters extended before his dazzled eyes. He leapt into a boat anchored there. Amid the bewildered silence over the waves, in which not even the vibration of a breeze sang, a voice that seemed to come from the heart of the waters said: "The undines are dominant, but the egregores of respiration are still less redoubtable than your own desire."

There was a happy assembly in the garden of delights. The young man perceived seven beautiful young women. They were divinely naked. One detached herself from the group and came to meet him. He seemed to remember having always loved her.

"Young man," she asked, "what have you come to seek in our retreat?"

The timbre of her voice evoked hours of joy. Troubled, he replied: "I believe that I've come to see you. Are you not Marie-Morgane, the singer of the sea, whose marvelous name men murmur anxiously?"[3]

She smiled like hope. "Yes, you recognize Morgane. Our races differ; I am not born of a woman. Fishermen, it is said on earth, see me surging from the foam of the waves, and the coppery planet respires to the rhythm of my bosom. You have come to us because you were elected. We expected your footfalls."

The young man looked at her with eyes of violent desire. She laughed like a woman.

---

[3] *Marie-Morganes* are marine fays akin to sirens, featured in Breton legend, the equivalent of the welsh *morgens*. The name and the legend were popularized in the 1870s by the folklorist François-Marie Luzel, who connected them with the myth of the drowning of the city of Ys.

"Here, we are not in the land from which you emerge," she said. "Since you are our guest, would you care to submit to our customs?"

"My will is the obedient daughter of yours."

All the gracious creatures of the garden surrounded the young stranger. Morgane picked a sumptuous flower.

"In the blue calyx of this flower you will respire the forgetfulness of your superfluous desires and all the events that have, in the past, inflicted wounds on the expansion of your desire. Have you suffered? By virtue of seeing your youth, men would say that you only have only known childish troubles. Perhaps they were cruelly sharp. Even when your days were dressed with exceptional benediction, they elapsed in the atmosphere of the earth, in which the universal dolor of life palpitates. Your childish eyes have wept. Your adolescent heart has swollen. Your human soul has been injured by the expectations of the future, brandishing, among the sheaf of its conjectural threats, the certainties of decadence and death.

"Inhale from the blue flower, friend, the forgetfulness of having suffered. Inhale also the forgetfulness—so precious also—of having diverted the forces of your soul toward furtive contingencies, foreign to your ideal. Inhale along with forgetfulness, friend, the power to live uniquely for your essential desire. Then you will walk here in joy and plenitude. But I can only give you the virtue of a momentary forgetfulness. I am offering you a truce in the consciousness of your destiny. I cannot inculcate the forgetfulness of your native instinct without drying up the sources of your life. Bonds of your anteriority attach you to it, incrusted within you so profoundly that I could not break them without tearing your flesh. One day, therefore, you will quit us."

"What madman would renounce the fatherland of his joy?"

"All men, for none is able to remain faithful to the miracle of his conquered ideal. You can depart whenever you wish. We only ask you not to take anything away from our insular homeland: not one flower, not one blade of grass. Will you make that oath?"

"I swear it. Superfluous words, in any case, for I shall never leave of my own will."

"We are not of the world of the earth, you see. That which surrounds us ought not to penetrate here."

With a mild gesture, he beautiful creature held out the blue flower, as blue as distantly virginal seas, and the young man was intoxicated by the perfume. The flower withered.

"Will you die of my kiss, friend flower?" he exclaimed. "Oh, adorable flower whose breath has cleansed my soul, lustral flower of forgetfulness, savior flower of primordial innocence, can I not weep now, to honor your loss?"

"One dies in giving one's soul," said Morgane, "and your amour is a partial death. From the heart of the initiatory corolla was drawn the birth of your life. For us, you date from the moment when you inhaled its supreme effluence. Receive the name that signifies your new soul: you will be called Adgan,[4] for you are reborn.

---

[4] Author's note: "Adgan in Celtic has the same significance as the Latin *renatus*." *Adgan* does appear in William Owen's Welsh dictionary, and in contemporary Breton dictionaries, but is not thus defined is either instance (*renatus* means reborn, and is echoed in the English word renascent). It is possible that the author is confusing it with the Arabic name

The days went by, florid with equal joy. Adgan was astonished to be happy.

The beautiful Marie-Morgane had a distant smile.

"Men are not born for happiness," she said. "All those to whom we have given it have borne it as a burden."

"For me it has the weight of a rose."

"You were exceptionally robust among men, and stronger of soul, but you can no longer carry a rose for an hour at the end of your extended arm, not contain perfect serenity for any longer without running out of breath. The light air of the virgin summits oppresses the breast of the children of men."

Applying its iridescent osculation to the flowery stems of the garden, a rainbow lost its curve in the distant limpidity of the sky.

"Look!" said Morgane, extending her diaphanous hand. "It's the sumptuous arch of the bridge that guides our desires to the shore of their blossoming."

She was delectably grave, like felicity. Pearls of dew were entangled in the somber waves of her hair, enlivening the warm dullness of her flesh, the vessel of a marvelous blood. A coppery gauze revealed her young body, emanating mysterious aromas. A feminine flower of a supreme world, Adnan contemplated her with his glad gaze, and although that country had abolished within him the effort of thought, he wondered, in sparse remembrance of the lost past, what that creature and her domain were for him.

Adnan, found in the Quran and said to refer to an individual who exists, or has existed, in two worlds or on two planes.

"Perhaps I am only the diapason of your hope," Morgane enunciated.

The young man shivered. His silence, however, was understood by the strange stroller, whose limpid radiance no anxiety could eclipse. She went on: "Why are you astonished, friend? It is not difficult to understand the thoughts of men, silent or sonorous, for the cage with which its wings collide is narrow. Like the others, are you unable to welcome joy without seeking its causes? What does the source matter of the river that bathes you with the delight of its waves? Look around you, soul as yet unquiet. An occult circle surrounds you, which cannot be crossed by morbid vampires, the entities of shadow generated by your thoughts of old, your irrevocably forgotten thoughts. The obscure satellite that follows your human footsteps, diminished brother of the one that saddens in the heavens the wake of the earth, ought to suspend its heavy fidelity to your tracks. Oh, breathe voluptuously the free air of these days. How you will regret later the possession of these present hours!"

"Forgive me, delectable and good friend. Humans are not accustomed to joy. It astonishes me as much as it intoxicates me."

"And you dream about its secret. Poor dreamer, what would you do with it? Do you think that you could create around this point, by your own strength, a world adequate to yourself?"

She indicated a splendid and solitary flower, on a branch of a bush, which launched forth more majestically than that of a tulip-tree. Its broad nacreous petals were as flamboyant as amorous pupils. No man could have perceived it without shivering.

"Look at that flower. It hides a marvelous secret in its calyx. The perfume that evaporates from it does not diminish by its intensity the mystery enclosed in its heart. Here, it is the symbol of joy. Anyone who plucked it in order to carry to the earth would only find a withered stem in his hand. Here, see with what fortunate grace it is allied with the forms that surround it. Do you not sense that here, like that flower, you are looking at your own reflection, your own correspondence? The happiness that my sisters and I are offering you is a world similar to yourself. See how the aspect of things accords with your beauty. Joy belongs to a man strong enough to invoke a world faithful to his precise ideal. Child, your debilitated hand does not have the strength for such work. We, the mysterious sisters, have collected you, a passive passer-by abandoned to yourself, in order to introduce you into the smiling creation of your primordial desires. Can you not contemplate here, charmed, the multiplied beauty of your soul, before your expanded eyes?"

She fell silent. Her sumptuous eyes followed visions. Light voices were singing, in the tender atmosphere, a hymn exalting the words of the dreaming beauty. Adgan sensed a mantle of joy on his shoulders.

If your feet ever land upon that fortunate island, passer-by, will you be able to contemplate without fatigue the reflection of your own beauty? Only heroes make that effort on human soil.

One night, Adgan was wandering in the marvelous garden. A soft light revealed the silent and perfumed landscape. The flowers raised themselves up like nocturnal lovers. Adgan passed before the majestic flower, fortified by an intoxicating secret, the great nacreous petals of which were flamboyant in the pale moonlight. He gazed at it, the flower wild with joy. He extended his audacious hand toward it. A sigh rose from his bosom. With a dry click, he snapped the stem, and then fled into the furtive night.

In the distant violet, a sad and superhuman voice sang: "If you pluck the flower of your hope from the earth, it will become poisonous and mortal."

One day, on human soil, passers-by found a pale young man lying on the ground, clutching a rotten stem in his clenched fingers. He woke up, and looked at his right hand and the decomposed flower vaguely. He was no longer able to speak; he was no longer able to smile. For a year he was perceived, a taciturn insensate whose gesture was tremulous. Then, one evening, the local children were frightened by stumbling over the cadaver of the familiar madman. It is said that there was an aura of strange light around his calm, handsome face. Death can also lead to the isle of joy, as to the ocean of despair and anguish.

THE DISTRESS OF HERCULES[5]

To Léon Dierx

The juvenile hero had hidden his forehead in the florid bosom of his lover, and she said: "What torment has expelled vagabond happiness from our hearts? Now that a heavy burden of unforeseen anguish has fallen upon our amour and corrupted it, the wings of kisses no longer rise up to the clouds, and the flower of joy is dead between our breasts. Dear soul, the eternal enemy, Destiny, has devastated our souls mysteriously. In mine, ashes have covered the flames, and desperately, I still sometimes embrace a corpse that my kisses cannot revive, the chimera of amour stifled in my arms. Our intimate past, which promised beautiful dreams, has only left us mortal chagrins. I loved your eyes, softer than my lies, so much!"

And the hero, whose thoughts were following their own path, replied in a bitter and desolate voice: "To you who were Amour, to you who were joy, I would only have harsh words. I have lost the star that guided me, the voice that called me toward the future has fallen silent; what sang within me of divine hope has fallen silent, and abandoned me, alone and defenseless. On the island of

---

[5] In *Contes surhumains* this story is rendered in verse of a sort, with an irregular rhyme-scheme and a variable scansion, which it did not seem necessary or profitable to retain in translation.

Desire where I am languishing, lost, I am the survivor of the Hero that I was, for I was born superb and proud. I am no more than a soul once great, but much diminished for having suffered too much beside your beautiful breasts. In my eyes, the starry gaze is extinguished, and my terrible strength is weary, extenuated for having fought the renascent rush of the vultures of Destiny, furious against our dreams."

Omphale said: "Over the hours of joy, always so brief, alas, the widespread wings of misfortune hover. The tortures that you have suffered because of me are an essential principle of your beauty. Your forehead will rise higher for having been tamed by the kiss of distress and woman; and I see you thus with a fearful heart, for I have sensed, confusedly, alive in your soul, a frightful force: my female weakness. I am afraid of your speech, as of the sea; I am afraid of entering into your interior thought, an unfathomable abyss in which my being is lost, a mysterious world in the depths of which dwells and abundant life, seething so forcefully that it is as vertiginous as death. Your intimate ideal, which I cannot comprehend, troubled my frail amour from all its height, and I believe I felt, when your beautiful head lay upon my bosom, that it would be able to charm, in returning to life, the burden of a sun falling upon my heart.

Hercules said: "O flower of my desire blossoming in woman, your body was for my eyes the form of hope. Hope is dead. Strength is dead. My once-powerful will is dead. And distress is eating into my sad amour, which was my last beauty. With the vertigo of your breath, I have sculpted, in the dream of loving you, the caryatid that that supports on the face of destiny the weight of my life. But everything has suddenly collapsed. Over my blind heart lucid intelligence hovers; and I am dying, a partial cadaver, for having modeled on a mortal ideal the immortal desire that burned in my loins."

Omphale said: "I lived on your breath, and I am a corpse. And even your soul is not strong enough to resuscitate my dead soul with love, a cadaver in which regret alone is alive. It is a chain of death that would link our loins, but the lily of your dreams has remained candid; do not allow it to wither under my arid breath. Go, depart, weary of pouring out the holy water of amour and life into a stillborn heart, too feeble to be born to your kiss. Go; the flight of an eagle with an arrow of its wing persists toward the sun! Raise your powerful bosom, the refuge of sad foreheads, where I also would have hidden my sad forehead in vain; raise its silhouette on the horizon of the world, like a temple enclosing in its profound beauty your ideal, radiant for hopeful hearts!"

And in the solitude of the evening, the Hero marched away, his hand replaced on the hilt of his sword. Launching his wounded gaze toward the heavens, he said: "I know that the hour will come when I shall extinguish my dream, but perhaps with dead arms, or so very weary."

SARDANAPALUS

To José-Maria de Hérédia

I have ventured, like little wanton boys that
swim on bladders, these many summers in a
sea of glory, but far beyond my depth, my
high-blown pride at length broke under me."
Shakespeare (*Henry VIII*, Act 3 Scene 2)[6]

(Words to the beloved)

Perhaps I am impotent to bend myself to the forms of life.

I could not renounce my ideal in order to adapt myself to an ambience, to make myself a beast of the herd, to become an individual considered by his contemporaries. Let others appear; for myself, I exist!

Passers-by brush me, a few speak to me and I reply; but I am far away from them. I live outside time. I am a foreigner in all fatherlands.

I could have assigned a unique goal to my existence and attained it: to conquer a part of the world, like Alexander or Napoléon; to create an eternal masterpiece, like Dante; to assembled talismanic gold, like Flamel. Cer-

---

[6] The uncredited quotation in the original is taken from a French translation, where Wolsey's soliloquy is abridged slightly. I have substituted the actual words of the text and added the credit.

tainly, I would have been able to furnish it, by means of one of those efforts. But in using up all their concentrated energies in a single ideal, Napoléon, Dante and Flamel only perceived life in one of its facets. I wanted more.

What more? To command the hearts of women, like Don Juan? To command the forces of nature, like Apollonius of Tyana? I have no doubt that it would be possible for me to accomplish what any other man, my fellow and my equal, could accomplish, for I was born to sit down in the council of heroes.

That is why I did not deign to choose, among my dreams, one whose pedestal I would have set on the soil of the earth. They are too numerous and variously beautiful. At least life has offered to my hope multiple and temporary flowers. I have glimpsed intimately varied aspects therein. I have been a nomadic Bohemian who did not built a roof in any homeland.

Among the memories with which I am opulent, there is one that I want to relate to you. One day, I was a weary, cruel and sad king. Now that I have entered the refuge of your arms, I will try to depict for you, for you who are purity itself, one of my bad dreams. And this story, which happened to me, I am writing in order to distract your mysterious eyes and your dear thought for one splenetic evening.

PART ONE

Scene I
Sardanapalus,[7] Iona

Nineveh, in the time of its glory: the hall in the royal palace is vast and high, profound and pensive in its sumptuousness; the polychromatic walls represent divine allegories. In a joyful sea-blue there is the mystical tree with seven branches from which a hero armored in gold is plucking the thorny fruits with a calm hand ; on another wall there is the genius whose who large wings, one ascending and the other descending, symbolize the double current of universal life.

Multicolored carpets strew the paving stones.

At the head of a mauve bed on which the king is sleeping, a colossal serancolin Cherub spreads his hieratic wings. The sibylline monster, whose human head, taurean wings, leonine feet and aquiline wings allegorize the quaternary of eternal knowledge, must be the tutelary guardian of Assur.

---

[7] Sardanapalus, who never actually existed, was the last king of Assyria, according to the highly unreliable Diodorus Siculus, allegedly quoting from a lost book by Ctesias. He was adapted by writers associated with the French and English Romantic Movements as a key symbol of ultimate decadence induced by ennui. An archetypal literary model was provided by Byron in the play *Sardanapalus* (1821), which bears no resemblance to the present text.

To the morning light that caresses the bright hori-
zon of woods dotted with pink flowers, the king wakes
up.

Sardanapalus is about thirty years old, a man of
powerful beauty. No garment attenuates the noble liberty
of his body. At first sight, he appears to be the blossom-
ing of a magnificent humanity. Studied in its details, his
form reveals a harmonious development that only the
rare elect of men attain: a type of which the metaphysi-
cal art of the Orient has transmitted the synthesis, un-
known to the Ionic statuary whose memory oppresses,
among Occidentals, the ideal of virile beauty; it differs
even more from the northern model, which races inatten-
tive to the graces of plasticity could not immortalize in
stone. Less cylindrical than the Greek figure, the form of
the man does not project the bulging planes of the north-
ern model.

The medium stature of the youthful sovereign is
slender, with the supple elegance of the lotus stems
sculpted amid the immemorial hieroglyphs. Over the
slim pelvis, the torso broadens as it rises toward the twin
frame of the pectoral muscles, into which the attach-
ments of the shoulders are lightly inserted. The precise
musculature is that of a being succeeded to the sumptu-
ous expansion of his energies. That exceedingly mascu-
line body has feminine gestures, the velvet movements of
a cat.

That contrast suggests a hint of imperfection in the
soul that is symbolized by that flesh, respiring noble
strength. The arms, marvelously modeled, are terminat-
ed by hands enlarged at the base of the thumb. But in its
heroic slenderness, the thumb, the revelator of the will,
stops. The skin of the young king is a fine white tissue
under which subtle pink network is visible at the joints.

41

The face is pale between the light brown curls and the annealed beard: the beauty of a nocturnal sky illuminated by starlight. The aquiline impression emanating therefrom reveals the wingspan of a desire as vast as a mainsail. Dominating the passionate line of the nose, lakes of indifference are displayed in the somber eyes, like those of an eagle with wounded wings, weary of the effort of walking on the ground. More than the other features, the wide, gravely voluptuous mouth is sealed by the planetary influx of Ishtar.

The king wears around his throat, maintained by a golden necklace, one of the seven talismans by means of which were summoned, by the force of incantations, the energies of the seven sacred planets.

On the couch that Sardanapalus has just quit, the youthful body of a sleeping woman reposes. She is a creature of grace and sensuality, a flower of delight whose breath seems light to respire on an evening of heavy life. An atmosphere of delights emanates from her gilded flesh, from her joyful breasts and her smiling lips.

The young man's eyes, lingering upon that charming form, gaze without seeing.

SARDANAPALUS

You are a pretty sleeping little beast, who can still perhaps give me joy, since the unique woman toward whom the august dream of my adolescence summoned me has not come. How light it is, the sleep that possesses your breast! Toward what prey is the hummingbird of your desire flying? Toward what pink flower or fickle ribbon? The irony of life! You, a child, not much more than a thing devoid of soul, can bind my pride for an hour with the chain of your frail arms, and disturb my life with the hope of a spasm upon your flesh! Repose, little body, like a lake gilded by moonlight. You are the lake on which the vessel of my dream lingers, which once departed in order to attain the stars of the horizon, and is now broken down in the pool where the pink lotus of your kiss blossoms. Repose in the aureole of your victory. Do you have the right to any pride, though? A living being has no other glory than that of the idea whose symbol it incarnates, but in its fugitive flight the eagle displays the pride of being crimson-tinted by the setting sun. You are the other pole of all that I have renounced. You are a fragment of my disaster.

(*At the bitter tone of those final words, the young woman, Iona, wakes up. With a pretty gesture, which seems to be pursuing the flight of a dream, she puts her arms around the king.*)

IONA

Have you slept well by my side, my sweet master? Show me your eyes, that I might see reflected therein the memory of your recent thoughts... Alas, your eyes have no smile for me, and your brow is obsessed by a chagrin that I do not know.

SARDANAPALUS

Oh, don't let the reflection of my cares trouble the limpidity of your childlike heart. And don't take off the gilded veil of your native joy, if you want to keep a little of it to envelop my head.

IONA

I would like my presence to be a perpetual kiss. Since you have selected me among the young women to intoxicate me with your caresses, since I possess your

43

royal beauty, my sole dream is to seem a nest of sensual pleasures, warm enough to consume the demon that haunts you. Oh, if I knew that you were happy, I would live in a heaven rose-tinted forever by the memory of your lips.

SARDANAPALUS
You who speak thus, like a gentle slave, like a flower become woman in order to be a lover, know that my speech has no virtue over destiny, but I want my desire to expand over your life like the cool shadow of a palm tree.

IONA
You have perfumed my life with joy in traversing it. I would like it not to belong to you, my handsome king, in order to be able to give it to you.

SARDANAPALUS
Be careful of reckless prayers. Do we know what I will make of you? Do you claim to know me? Child, child, my heart is obscure to my own eagle eyes; do not try to see into it! I would have liked to pass through the company of beings while retaining an innocent voice and pure hands, but ferocious beings might sleep within me whose claws sometimes spread over hearts.

(The king lies down on the vast mauve bed, his head supported by his right hand. He speaks as if, unknown to him, his thought is putting on the sonorous envelope of his voice, and his eyes do not see Iona, who is looking at him anxiously, pursuing with the force of her feminine intuition her lover's tenebrous dream.)

SARDANAPALUS

Iranian merchants have often brought me captive lions, and I have seen the gazes of those magnificent animals, so similar to mine—oh, those gazes, in which the reflection of invisible horizons quiver!—that I have returned those sad lions to the beauty of the desert and the open horizons surcharged with vertigo. But who will liberate me? What man, or what archangel, will open the doors to me through which I can escape to the shores of which I have the presentiment? Oh, to live another life, powerful and sweet, that I have suspected in fugitive lightning flashes of vision! Once, I desired to change the appearances of my life, but it no longer interests me to amuse a minute of my fantasy with that play. At this moment, somewhere on earth, a man is going naked, powerful and calm, possessing nothing but his strength and his pride. Resplendent in his insouciant face is the joy of living in fidelity to his instinct, harmonious amid the harmony of the world, abandoned to the rhythm of beautiful appearances I would like to be that man. Is my will not able to reject the past, as a tree surrenders to the wind in order to shake of its fruits? Yes, I would like to be that man. But I would still remain a man. And the arrow of my desire is aimed at a more distant target.

(*Abruptly, the king turns to the young woman, who is trying to follow the royal imagination with her tender blonde eyes.*)

If I were to put my life in your hands, what would you do with it?

IONA

I would make it my joy, in order to try to make it yours.

SARDANAPALUS

Speak to me, speak to me! I often need to hear the singing babble of a woman, which caresses, like the light flight of bees, the black efflorescence of my thought.

IONA

Listen, then, my sad lover, for I no longer know whether it is me who is speaking. In the life of every woman, a moment comes when all the tenebrous treasure of her being is suddenly manifest clearly. And I sense that the hour of my destiny is sounding now. Look at me, my beloved, for it will vanish forever, this fugitive moment of my beauty. Certain trees die after their unique flowering. Now, in this solemn passage of time, can you sense all the flower of myself exhaling its supreme perfume toward your heart? Can you hear in my voice, which astonishes me, some invisible demon singing, joyful and tender, of which I am, in the other hours of my existence, only the unconscious and pale slave. To you, prince of my powers, I am to bring the mystery of sensual pleasure. Look at me: my body is desirable, and as fugitive as the moon. Listen to me: my voice is murmuring as seductively as southerly breezes in swooning palm trees, as authoritatively as the incantations of mages. Inhale me: an insinuating aroma emanates from my breasts like those of the countries of which one dreams. Envelop me with your arms: my embrace is as warm as sunlight. And come to taste on my lips a flavor more violent than the fruits of the mystical tree with seven branches. Come toward my gilded loins as toward your homeland!

(*Motionless in his attitude of a wild beast in repose, whose eyes alone are moving, Sardanapalus has followed simultaneously her thought and the music of her speech, coming from much further away than the gracious mouth that proffers them and the amiable soul by which they are furrowed.*)

SARDANAPALUS
Destiny, the god whose breath curbs flames toward the ground, engenders daughters with sweet voices on earth.

IONA
Come toward my enlacement, in which all cares die. Come: you will live the long triumph of your youth and your strength, and you will be the true king, sacred by virtue of kisses.

SARDANAPALUS
(*starting, with a sudden release of his entire self.*)
Shut up! I can only talk any longer to the gods!

A man (*entering on these words.*)

So be it! I am listening.

Scene II
Sardanapalus, Arad-Anu, then the jester Rabitou

(*That man, the prince of Ninevite mages, Arad-Anu, is in the prime of life. He seems made to remain there forever. One might think him a human representation of incessantly renewed strength. A white silk robe striped with broad golden fringes, which flow capriciously around his legs and his loins, is wrapped around his body, free of superfluous gestures. He has eyes of a tranquil audacity and an invincible youth, which never weary of the effort of having contemplated mysterious ideas.*

At the entrance of that individual, the king has shuddered like a warhorse at the sound of fanfares. Iona has fled, like a dove alarmed by the flight of an eagle.)

ARAD-ANU
Your young pride bounds like a drunken goat. But its audacity pleases those whose daring goes beyond pride.

SARDANAPALUS
Proud, me! Do even I know where I am? My vision of myself is sometimes red and sometimes gray. I admire myself and deplore myself. But no one loves me.

ARAD-ANU
Child, what effort have you made, to admire in yourself?

SARDANAPALUS
That of living.

ARAD-ANU
Glorify yourself, then in a work accomplished by men and pigs alike!

SARDANAPALUS

Would I not be dead already if I renounced my last hope?

ARAD-ANU

Your last hour is inscribed in the book of Destiny. Do not believe that you can scratch it out with your feeble gesture? A man is killed by his vice. You will die of pride.

SARDANAPALUS

Do you take me for a child that a specter can frighten? Oh, when it comes toward my bosom, with what joy will I salute death!

ARAD-ANU

If they did not know how to die, what would remain, then, to those who are unskillful in living?

SARDANAPALUS

You know me, Master, better that I shall ever know myself. I was not born to live. Oh, even when tender goddesses would have bathed my heart in an atmosphere of joy...but will I ever know who I am?

ARAD-ANU

If you knew yourself, you would also know the universe and the gods, all the way to their very source.

SARDANAPALUS

I often see myself, magnificent and superhuman, intoxicated by having conquered, over the double hostility of life and death, a flamboyant ideal of eternity. Then, at times, I feel that I am a helpless infant that a pale evening breeze could annihilate. At that hour, when the intoxication of being ebbs away from my brow, listen: I am the flower of a race. In the darkness of centuries, slow generations have nourished with their tears the sap from which my presence sprang forth. Oh, how they toiled, those sad ancestors turned to dust, in order that their effort would project over the earth their obscure ideal, revealed in my beauty! And here I am, surging over their past anguish like a conqueror armored in gold over the bloody flesh of battles.

ARAD-ANU

If mysterious wills, human and superhuman, were propitious to the advent of your glory, if they made of you, not some limited king of a limited country, but a real prince among men, do you believe that they would demand nothing more of you than that you contemplate yourself in a mirror, by the vacillating torchlight of your pride?

SARDANAPALUS

Is it not enough, then, to appear down here, haloed with the reflection of divine forces? In the balance in which the archangels weigh human incidents, the essential pride of my youth prevails over an accumulation of ugly and ignominious things. I see in my beauty the redemption of the foreign hideousness from which I suffer. Look at me, you who penetrate the language of forms. On my youthful and strong body you will see—the vestiges of frightful kisses—the memory of splendid ideas that summoned my incantation. I have made my bosom the ark of a magnificent dream, and I have launched the tumultuous army of my desires to conquer an absolute. The enchained Cherub follows my footsteps in the desert of the world, for, by a distant predestination. I do not only commend human populations. I order the quaternary forces and I understand the voice of silence. In the eternal mirror in which the reflection of beings resides forever, have I not imprinted my image as a human type radiant with glory?

ARAD-ANU
Continue, child; I am indulgent.

SARDANAPALUS
You have suffered, then?

ARAD-ANU
I no longer remember.

SARDANAPALUS
Ah! When the waters of death have cleansed my heart, will they suffice to efface all the bites of past sufferings? Your speech has strange powers, Master. It has struck me down on the summit to whim my pride had elevated me. Oh, misery; here I am, reduced to a sad child, fearful of destiny and scorned by your gaze. And if you do not turn away from the audacious dreamer your face, which lodged conquered serenity, may you bear away my weakness!

ARAD-ANU
To those who have crossed the seven circles of anguish, a man's anxiety is sacred.

SARDANAPALUS
But do you know yourself all the suffering than can gnaw a breast other than your own? Do you know all the

anguish of my sleepless nights? Can you measure what there is in my soul? No more than a man can land alive on the pale shores of the moon can he penetrate the mystery of another human being. Do you know…?

ARAD-ANU

I know everything that the eyes say, everything that the forms sing.

SARDANAPALUS

Broken impulsions; the efforts of wings brutally broken by the unspeakable Adversary, resorbed expansions; murdered powers; vain forces; it is your lamentable procession that is guiding my life toward its becoming, like a troops of mutilated lions preceded by their sad pastor. What does it matter? Only those who attempt the summits are cast down. My past only counts defeats. But is not destiny an enemy before which a man can fall without shame?

ARAD-ANU

You have no other enemy than yourself. The road that leads to superhumanity is dolorous, and strewn with gulfs. You have ascended one slope of the sacred mountain. Standing on the summit, gaze at the slope that will bring you back, prince of the superhuman secret, toward your definitive place amid human life. You were not born, child, for perpetual solitude. There you would allow yourself to be invaded by darkness, excessively pale candle! The planets that smiled upon your birth did not consecrate you to the tranquility of a sage but to the assault of the passions; it is up to you to guide them, a flock quivering with beauty, toward the conquest of your ideal, the reflection of which might charm humans. Your past weighs heavily upon your shoulders, son of destiny. Shake off that burden in order to extend your hand freely toward your future, engendered by a kiss of your will on the mouth of a providence. Recreate your initial word and throw it into the balance of the world. Think that your name might become a talisman, investing with a force the mouth that pronounces it. Think that you can give sumptuous substance to all your virtual pride, the cortege of which might carry you high into the certain skies of eternal hope.

SARDANAPALUS

Can your speech pour life into my agonizing will? Alas, no. We are both outside life. Fatally impassioned, I see into my last hope as into a tomb. You, mage, live outside nature, beyond the turbulence of appearances, beyond the efflorescence of adorable forms, an immanent statue in the niche of an orb of eternity. Is there still a heart in your breast, a heart whose speech might perhaps save me?

ARAD-ANU

You have no other savior but yourself. Escape your incomplete pride, intermittent demigod, since you cannot maintain yourself in the igneous calyx of supreme pride. There are, in fallen races, women whose pride refuses the august gesture of the kiss, sad women, accursed in their loins, which do not give life. Like them, you are sterile and lamentable, because your pride has lost the audacity of conquering its exact place in the harmony of the world, a disorbited star that will lose its light in its fall.

SARDANAPALUS

At least there will remain to me a beauty of darkness. Oh, you rebels whose glorious spines were broken by the refusal to bend, rebels distributed on every step of all the stairways rising to the heavens, fallen archangels, blasted demigods, heroic aggressors of fatalities, men contemptuous of life, all of you have agony for a companion, you in whom I sense sad brethren, you whose proud anguish resonates in the depths of my entrails. Will I always be similar to you, solitaries vanquished by destiny? O noble mouths that project by turns the pure breath of hymns and the spittle of blasphemy toward the divine night, have I not sensed on my flesh a robe of fire woven of your fraternal kisses?

(*With a vehement gesture, the king seizes with full clenched hands the flesh of his breast, as if to tear away from it a devouring envelope of flames. Then he paces, with long, rapid strides, brushing the walls, as if in a prison from which escape seems impossible. Now his shoulders are enveloped in a long robe of green silk, on which copper filigree embroiders occult characters. At the level of his nipples a heavy golden pin dotted with carbuncles designs a solar hieroglyph.*

Outside, a shrill and jovial singing voice draws nearer.)

THE VOICE OF THE JESTER RABITOU
Try to make of your soul
The procuress of your desire,
And know how to kiss life
Like a woman.

SARDANAPALUS

Voice from below, voice that mocks and sullies, how are you able to sing at this complicit hour? Diabolical song of a jester mocking beauty, how can you still move the stagnant mud in my breast? Laughter, sinister laughter, lame son of discord, persecutor surging forth when harmony disappears, as nightmares come running after the flight of light, laughter saddened by feigning joy, how many times you have wounded my soul!

THE JESTER RABITOU

Do you desire that I make your pretty little whore of a soul, which spends its life gazing at itself in a mirror, appear to your proud eyes?

SARDANAPALUS

(*to himself.*)

If you want to climb higher, you will fall back that much further. If your flight pursues the stars, beware of your imminent fall, into some depth of mud. Norm of reaction, into what gulf will you hurl me?

THE JESTER RABITOU

There she is, my amiable little son, there she is, the slut that you cherish, your image and your essence. Oh, I know her, as the nurse knows her shit-stained doll; I scent her as dogs scent the reek of the tomb on old made-up women. Yes, my son, have you ever seen an aged prostitute fluffing herself up for a fête? That's your soul, your dear little slattern of a soul and your idolatry. A russet wig on her bald head, enamel on her skin, as flabby as an empty waterskin, black around the eyes and carmine on the mouth, heightened by a beauty spot, with an iron corset shoring up the tits hanging down over the belly in cascades. Thus prettified, she will simper before her mirror, where her slack lips will want to kiss themselves recklessly, with a sonorous collision of the gold of false teeth against the silver of the mirror. And that is the figurative symbol of the beautiful soul of my sovereign lord, is it not, Master great mage Arad-Anu?

ARAD-ANU
(*to Sardanapalus*)
You ought to listen to him. Even the face of a god can be reflected in a grimace on the illusion of a disordered sky. Truth is differentiated in error, beauty in ugliness, through the prism of weak minds.

(*He leaves.*)

SARDANAPALUS
Yes, go on, fool, continue on your twisted path. Your voice pours forth the bitter joy of depressing poisons. There is a savage sensuality in seeing one's intimate debility multiplied in the baseness of another, hearing one's own voice deformed in the eruptions of a perverse echo, of smelling the odor of a rotten ideal in an ignoble breath.

THE JESTER RABITOU
Is my breath rotten, my little son? So is yours, then, with a gangrene drawn from the same source, the same female interior. A poor fool truly needs to be patient to support your fits of pretentious nonsense every day and your air of a melancholy cuckold. Do you know that royal contact is injurious to the modesty of clowns? With you, I'd end up trading the gaiety of my estate for the conceited pride of yours, and I'd become proud of

sometimes favoring the acquaintance of pimps and prostitutes, all the more so as you encourage the entry of young men into brothels, the money of the poor into the pockets of the rich and steel blades into human flesh—which incontestably constitutes the triple fundamental function of all royal, imperial, sacerdotal or republican power. But don't worry, I'm not infatuated with anything, not even the fact that you aren't my cousin, for if I became vain and pompous, I'd become as tedious as your august and solemn person, which is why you'd project mine far from here with a kick up the backside, given that nothing is as irksome as finding one's own resemblance in others.

SARDANAPALUS
Have no fear of that, vile clown. You're linked to me by a solid chain; the evocation of the vile world swarming with brutality, mockery and vulgarity. No cortege of heroes had passed over the earth without contemplating heroism, and your presence is perhaps as bitterly necessary to me as that of evil spirits and sinister councilors.

RABITOU
So, for once in your life you've said something sensible. By hanging out with fools, men become wise. If you got away from metaphysical nonsense, you could show yourself to be an honorable pedant. Yes, we're old allies, old accomplices. Here, take your scepter, the proud staff of a pastor of men.

SARDANAPALUS
Do you think I'd dishonor it by whipping your back with it?

RABITOU

Not so fast, my grandson. Take your scepter. Here's my bauble in my right hand; and the two of us can make an assault with sticks, the sticks with which we strike the world semipiternally. See this bauble, and salute it courteously with your scepter. The shaft is wood, harder than a twenty-year-old's phallus; the doll who surmounts it, skirted in silk, quercitrine and zinzoline, enlivened by little bells, rings as joyfully as the laughter of a woman who has just cuckolded her husband. If your scepter strikes my bauble in the encounter of a parade, you'll hear it more loudly, the obsessive ringing whose echo is prolonged beyond your ears to mock your effort, your energy, your attack and your defense. Head, banderole or flanconade? Go on—a jester's blows always carry. His bauble is a tintinnabulating club, and the day when his bells lose their clear sonority there will be mourning on earth, and the world will end.

SARDANAPALUS

The end of the world! That will come when no soul will any longer have amour.

RABITOU

Or rather when, jesters like me having disappeared, all that will remain are philosophers like you. In any case, you irritate me by a little treating my laughter with scorn. By pricking the hearing, it deflates the blister of your pride. In spite of your ambitious pride, you're only similar to others. If a clown weren't there to laugh at you, and everybody else, the world would become too stupid, too pretentious and too insipid—an excess that would lead to its end. Think how bored you'd all be if I didn't exist. Imagine a country in which all the passers-by would be leather bags in which were accumulated all the stupidity of a soldier, the rascality of a magistrate and the hypocrisy of a priest, further adulterated by the solemnity of a hippopotamus, a schoolmaster and the mother superior of a brothel. People are an abscess that laughter punctures, and that's why one dies laughing.

SARDANAPALUS

(*to himself.*)

Ignoble speech, then, flows together with sublime speech by the magic of the proffered word. So the fellow that is down below speaks like the one on high, for the miracle of a similar realization. The dungheap down below, the breath of the sun on high: that's what gives birth to the splendor of the rose. And the voice of the jester awakes in my memory that if the mage: "Your enthusiasm will only be a forced of destruction if you cannot situate it within the universal harmony. What is the good of creating a god in yourself if you cannot assign him his place at the feet of the primordial god?" Oh, I've listened too much to the beating of my heart to hear the rhythm of life. Now, here comes that wretched clown to reveal humility to me.

RABITOU

Do you take me for a pedant, then? My naïve pleasure in mocking you will be spoiled if it pleases you to accord me in your mind the license of a pedagogue. I call a pedant any man who imagines a utility at the end of the role he plays in this world, at the breakdown of what he spouts while chattering at hazard. My glory is to be as devoid of utility as the song of the nightingale, a flower devoid of sex or a beautiful girl who dies a virgin.

When my carcass is nailed between four planks, people will cry above it: "Here lies a fool," and over yours, "Here lies a king, a master of men!" And with that, a long panegyric sufficiently stuffed with lies. For, my poor child, you won't be able to do anything, even when dead, since, in order to fan the flame, it's necessary to be a fool, a philosopher or in love, or a poet—which is to say, to possess all three qualities of which you'd strive in vain to acquire the slightest. Then again, perhaps people will esteem you a fool. In that case their unlimited stupidity would be decorating you with an unmerited honor.

Scene III
Sardanapalus, The Poet

SARDANAPALUS

Come, young man invested with the solar breath, be welcome, for, in order to live, the world needs your speech, the echo of its own conscience. And I am not, alas, stronger than the world. Speak, you whose voice inspires strength and casts down the prisons in which human weakness languishes. Speak, you who were initiated not by men but by gods, you whose tongue is blessed with divine sincerity. I have found in your songs the multiple vibrations of my being. Your voice has revealed angels asleep within me. In sublime evenings I have lived the enchantment of embracing the catholicity invoked by your rhythms, the quivering mystery of incarnating oneself in a form of beauty, and your thought possessed my soul as a lover possesses a woman and fecundates her.

It is the spirit of the gods, it is the eternal word that sings, not your lips. Your wide open eyes see the integral secret and you paint the vision by which you remain dazzled. The human rabble only pierces the fugitive appearances of the world; you alone penetrate its reality, to motivation and its essence. It seems such as the crowd perceives it; it is as you sing it, and that is why the vulgar proclaim that you are hallucinated. The mole denies the sight of the lynx. I am only a powerful king, a lord of bodies, a prince of vain things. You are an emperor of souls, and I shall listen to you, Master, with the quivering joy of predestined children. Like every living being, and among the most impetuous, I have clamored toward happiness with the ardent lungs of my youth. I promise half my empire to whoever can bring a plenitude of joy to the world, in order that I can play my part therein, since there is no individual happiness. You who can dress breasts with a kind of enthusiasm, can you tell me the secret of being happy?

THE POET

Have you forgotten everything, then? The virtue of a secret vanishes with its halo of silence, evaporates in the wound of its divulgence, like the perfume of an uncorked bottle. An arcanum is a flower of darkness, which dies at the first kiss of sunlight. If I gave you the supreme secret of being happy, what would you be able to do with it?

SARDANAPALUS

You speak like a king. I have spoken like a child. It is sometimes a stranger that I hear in the voice that escapes my lips. Your forehead exhales the serenity of the strong. Against the disgust of being, what ideal has armored your breast?

THE POET

I have kept it naked, but full of love.

SARDANAPALUS

For a woman?

THE POET

Even limited by the arms of a woman, amour is sufficient for the glory of a life. Of all the cups that a man raises to his lips, the love of a woman is one of the purest, since he drinks suffering therein.

SARDANAPALUS

So be it. That is one of the illuminations with which I have flagellated my soul.

THE POET

Awaken, in the silence of your memory, the adorable evening when the mystery of the kiss was awakened in you. If you did not love the woman who first opened the sanctuary of her loins to your youth, think what your ecstasy would have been in embracing the eternal bride of your dream. Doubtless you would have sensed, amid the vertigo of the first hour, the wing of death gliding over your forehead, which hovers over every great joy.

SARDANAPALUS

Ah! So you have known that indescribable ecstasy toward which my arms are extended desperately?

THE POET

Look at me, then. You will see another radiation on my face. If I had savored that ecstasy, would you be talking to me now? It alone would have populated my life. O dazzling dream of adolescent evenings, I resigned my-self precociously to renouncing your possession.

SARDANAPALUS

I feel sorry for you, then; for to renounce one's de-sire it to expose one's heart to the most violent bites of that same desire. If you wanted to die ascetic to the joy of life, it is because the mirage of its distant flames burned in your blood. Renunciation is nothing but the gesture of a frantic passion. You do not resist a vertigo unless it attracts you.

THE POET

The phoenix dies in order to live again more glori-ously. If I have renounced the joys of the earth, it is in order to drink the essence more deeply. All the beauties of the world, which do not frighten any effort of my arms toward their embrace, come to inscribe their reflec-tion powerfully in my soul, as the sky is reflected more intensely in the sea.

SARDANAPALUS

Perhaps you are only a poor man unskillful in liv-ing, taking refuge in the sterile islet of your reverie and devoured by hunger for fruits of the earth ripened far from your feeble hand, and you charm with the air of a flute the regret of not having unmuzzled your passions to the prey down here. You go forth singing your life? Would you like to live it? Would you like to wrap your-self in a flap of my royal mantle, and would you like all of the joys that you have not bitten and of which I am weary?

THE POET

Offer diamond dust to someone who possesses a star. Of the three joys that life tolerates: the woman beloved, the idea conceived and the force of enthusiasm, which do you have the power to give?

SARDANAPALUS

Ah! No living being can give a joy to another. Oh, carnival king and masquerade poet! Derision of two augural majesties confronted by the most anxious impotence! You cannot communicate the arcanum of happiness to me; I cannot confer any joy on you. Oh, solitude, solitude of all! Between one being and another, an uncrossable desert extends, and what can one soul do for another?

THE POET

It can love it.

SARDANAPALUS

When it is superhuman.

THE POET

Simply when it is alive.

SARDANAPALUS

Friend, mine is dead. The permanent power to love does not reside in a royal bosom. That of which I was the intermittent depository has abandoned me. An aerie in which no eagle any longer nests is nothing but a hole in a stone. A man emptied of amour is nothing but a cadaver. Do you believe me to be alive?

THE POET

Yes, since you're suffering.

SARDANAPALUS

Your eyes are not seeing. I tell you that my soul is dead. Perhaps the world is nothing for the soul but the six walls of a tomb. Mine is dead, I tell you, and theurgy with trembling hands, the last hope born of it, is incanting its scabrous resurrection in vain.

THE POET

The dead resuscitate. They have changed the form of their life. No death is an end.

PART TWO

(*Sardanapalus is alone on the terrace of the palace. The warm night is descending over the city. Glimmers are ignited in several planes of the darkness. The earth exhales a breath of sensuality. The silence of the stars flows over humans. In the west, sheaves of fire spring from the temple of universal Ishtar. Light and music are coming from there, because, on one of the terraces, the sacred courtesans are singing a hymn to Lust:*)

O Lust,

You whose breath of flame penetrates the body like the emprise of lightning; Queen of fecund loins, queen of sterile loins; mother from whose heart emanates inextinguishably, the kisses that cause screams, the caresses that cause death; consoling sister of the distress of life; goddess with the abyssal eyes, lover with breasts of lava, Lust, be blessed in time and space!

O Lust,

Humans go forth, seeking happiness by various paths. All of them lead to the gulf of the impossible without you, august Lust. Arms extended toward the heavens will never embrace dreams. But they grasp, bewildered to sense a flux of flame in their veins, panting and tensed flesh. The purest enthusiasms break their flight upon the rock of despair. Only the vertigo of spasms bears hearts away to the heart of the gods.

O Lust,

Sacred Lust, you reign over the candid animals, which, magnificently obedient to your force, make gestures of amour beneath the eyes of the sun. The sexual worlds fornicate in the ether. The blue cteis of the stars gapes toward the phallus of suns without number, quivering like the pistils of lilies beneath the golden rain of pollen.

O Lust,

There are no gods without blasphemy. Some insult you, and trample underfoot your crown of bloody roses. But that hatred is only the rebellion of amour. Pale ascetics, and the spinsters who due in the cold perfume of virginity, have only renounced you because they have been bewildered by your vertigo. And their negative dream is fascinated by your fiery image.

O Lust,

A curse upon anyone who curses you, O mistress of human beings, the sole flower plucked in the meadow of desires. You, shepherd of the living, guide them toward death along paths of joy. You bear infinity in your quivering hands, and your lips are the cup of flame offering the glory of living in multiplied force.

O Lust,

Those ignorant of the Mystery believe that death will deliver them from your yoke. Vain hope! You dominate even more harshly the fatherland of the dead. O goddess similar to death. The first seven zones that the defunct of the earth traverse in the desire to be reintegrated with the immemorial Unity, you hold in your right. The turbulence of ankle-bones rolls sexual effluvia of an irresistible vehemence, and the man who, alive, sought God in the loins of a woman, will search for him in the wombs of lamia when dead.

O Lust.

Tell us, goddess: Have we penetrated all your arcana? Have the ancestors bequeathed us all the sciences of your virtue? Are there still inviolate mysteries in your sanctuaries? Are there new rites in your eternal worship? Oh, speak! Do you know sins that the earth has not committed? Will you inform us of warmer embraces and more forceful kisses?

O Lust,

You whose breath of flame penetrates the body like the emprise of lightning; Queen of fecund loins, queen of sterile loins; mother from whose heart emanates inextinguishably, the kisses that cause screams, the caresses that cause death; consoling sister of the distress of life; goddess with the abyssal eyes, lover with breasts of lava, Lust, be blessed in time and space!

SARDANAPALUS

Oh, lying voices! You lie as she does, O Lust, the most deceptive of smiles, malevolent alchemist who transmutes into sadness the promises of your joys. How many of my anterior brethren, noble among the sons of woman, have rushed their souls desperately toward your smile? Accomplice of the desert, your mirage attracts my gaze in vain. Warm voices of the night, you unfurl in vain toward my breast. Oh, rather strip away the lie of our ecstasy! Mourn impotent Lust, mourn also that impostor, human effort, and let your bloody hymns admit honestly to the stars the abortion of a beautiful hope of the earth!

THE VOICES OF THE COURTESANS
(*resuming in the distance.*)

Appear, then, as naked as truth, O Lust! And we shall tear the diadem from your hair, and we shall tear up the light mail of orphrey through which our lips desire the flowers of your bosom and the golden fleece of your pubis. Be naked, O lust, like a skeleton stripped of its flesh. Thus you are not beautiful! And that we have known as soon as our first contact. We have only loved you in despair, O somber queen whose real face is harsh to the kiss. Your strength, we are drunk from singing, and, annihilating the echo of our voices, the sacred silence informs us of our imposture. But what priesthood has not induced its pontiff to imposture? Fortunate is the man who can give the world a new lie!

SARDANAPALUS

And woe betide the man who brings it an eternal truth! But what does these sophisticated songs matter to me? Am I, a troubled child, going to allow foreign voices to enter into me? Am I not too solitary for the speech of another to be able to reverberate within me? Man, poor man of little strength, try to live your life and die in your own way, and assemble, for the incantation of your essential hope, the last forces that remain to you. Oh, if my soul has the power to engender, if my shade can inscribe on the wall of destiny, if my bosom is still magnetized by a little stellar force, let the projection of my voice etch, like *aqua fortis*, the copper of the future! O woman whom I could love, you ought, however, to hear my appeal. Why have you not yet come? Why are you not here? I know that you would come toward your lover, toward the man who is writhing in desire and dolor, in despair and hope, and who would live of your kiss, as others have died of it.

Come as if you were the form of my quivering and multiform desire, as if your flesh were kneaded by my tears, my sweat and my blood.

Come as if you were the astonished incarnation of all that I love in life; as if a wake spread out infinitely behind you of all the beauties of the visible an invisible world that have intoxicated my eyes; as if one of your two breasts were eternal Beauty and the other eternal Justice.

Come as if you were joy itself, the joy of which the excessively strong kiss perhaps leaves a bitter taste in our feeble souls.

Come as if your heart were steel and as if my breast were the magnetic mountain that rises at the world's Pole. You would come if you had to march barefoot over red hot iron spikes, if you had to fray a path by cunning or crime, if you had to lie to your ideal or kill the dog that loves you.

Come as if all those who have died of amour since the birth of the world were emerging from the tomb to throw you into my arms.

Come as if you were the smiling specter of an amour assassinated by its own violence.

Come as if you were the very statue of desired death, as if you were, beyond death, an immortal anguish, torture and despair.

(*At the last vibrations of his speech, the young man has shivered. In the depths of his being, a shock of reaction informs him that his incantation has not shaken in vain the stellar waves of the night.*)

(*Now, since that day, the days have flowed over the head of the king. Their number? What does it matter? Only hours of distress or hope count. It happens that the unknown woman to whom he appealed has come. How? What does it matter? Beings march toward one another*) *in accordance with the impulsion of ineluctable affinities.*)

SARDANAPALUS

Before your coming I believed that I was alive. Ignorance! On the balcony of death I watched life pass by. I still remember, in this century on this earth, wingbeats in a cavern in another age, on another world. That was me.

HELIBAH

I know no other thought than having waiting for your arms. I was a princess asleep in an immemorial slumber. Your lips have awakened me.

SARDANAPALUS

You are speaking of your past. It was my exile and my suffering. One always finds oneself too late. Before I saw you, everything that brushed you wounded me, everything that did you harm also oppressed me. Remember that my jealousy only attacks things of old. For I am jealous of the roses that charmed you, jealous of the hours of joy that inflated your breast, and jealous of the pain that kissed your mouth with its maw of red hot iron. Oh, if only nothing in the world had touched you, delightful child, and no eyelid had fluttered sensuously under the caress of your apparition. If only you had emerged from solitary limbo to enter into my arms immediately!

HELIBAH

There were years of me of which you are ignorant. The transfigurations of my beauty, the successive appearances of my being remain unknown to your amorous eyes. You have not seen my pink infancy and my mauve adolescence. My past is only a dead lily whose futile perfume has evaporated in an orb of solitude.

SARDANAPALUS
A perfume that occult breezes brought me in gusts of hope. In the aroma of summer nights, on which our breasts become sensible to the respiration on the earth, I recognized the breath of your life, of your strong and radiant life, a concentration of my expectations.

HELIBAH
At the bottom of the ocean there are marvelous flowers whose glory is unsuspected by any human eye. Thus, beneath the monotonous unfurling of the hours, splendors consecrated to secrecy flourished in me. I was a soul of election in a heroic form. But my beauty sang a hymn too powerful to be heard by men. The wings of my thought gave them vertigo, and my life has not revealed the mystery of my aspirations, the force of my virtualities. It seemed to me that my lips and my heart ought only to open to the kiss of a god. I have not walked naked, even in the desert, and my soul has enveloped itself in the silent pride of existence. Alas, my beloved, those blossomings of myself were lost to you.

SARDANAPALUS
No, for I dreamed you.

HELIBAH
In me you will not find a lover of joy. The urn of my heart is fragrant with melancholy. And into the rapture of your arms I bring the regret of sterile pasts. I would like it so much if no hour had touched us without

throwing us toward one another, if your life and mine had been confounded from birth to death, as our selves are during the kiss of our flesh.

SARDANAPALUS
Yes, in spite of our efforts, our hearts are heavy with the past. Our life on earth and our forgotten anterior lives, in other cycles, on other worlds, throw the weight of our chains over our impulsions of flight. Perhaps you, dear head can still have the flight toward amour of great frigates toward calm. I am afraid of being, for amour as for all beauties, an eagle with a broken wing.

HELIBAH
Do you not sense in me the strength to bind and un-bind. I will deliver you from all shackles. I only remember having hoped for you. I cannot lose you. And I will carry you away in my strong woman's arms, all the way to the stars of your desire.

SARDANAPALUS
Yes, although a woman, you will not cast any shadow over my ascendant, since you emanate from light. Yes, as soon as our approach, as soon as your first step toward my bosom, I felt your radiance exalting within me—supreme hope!—the beauty that slumbers there. Yes, you, you alone in the world, among beings, things and dreams, were not inferior to my desire, nor superior to my power. Salutations to the woman of my height! And your kiss remains the unique rose that I have collected in the garden of beautiful dreams. In the distant horizons of your bight eyes, I have discovered the country where the air is light for me, where the springs are fresh for me.

HELIBAH

Thus you sense rising within you the definitive faith in my work of amour, for which I was born. Yes, we will give to your kiss the conquering force, the force equal to the gods.

SARDANAPALUS

Your kiss will be supported by an image; for in order to receive it, I shall become the man adequate to his essential dream, the statue of my ideal.

HELIBAH

Amour only ever embraces images. It is exalted by enveloping its own creation. I love you; I have created you.

SARDANAPALUS

You have created me as I ought to be. Thank you! If I could not do it in the air of the earth, at least I will have been myself in the world of your heart. In the mirror of your delectable eyes, I see myself clad in glory, and your loins of joy are the pedestal from which my pantheistic figure springs. What does it matter that I have not cast upon the mud of this planet the exact shadow of my stature? In the palace of your heart I feel that I am the king. Everywhere, in any case, I was the solitary stranger pursued by the hostility of gazes, by the incomprehension of souls.

HELIBAH

Will I be able to remain at the height of your dream? Every flower of beauty fades, every flame is extinguished. Amour has the duration of a kiss from life to death. Perhaps one day you will be the beggar wandering among the ruins of the palace of my heart, a woman's fragile heart. And in the evening, the sad evening of life, our shades will wander, sad curbed shades, seeking, still seeking the debris of our beautiful memories, in order to build a new shelter therewith.

SARDANAPALUS

What does it matter? What does it matter, if we have extracted from the infinite matrix of eternity the gold decorating our lives? The adamantine hours of sublimity are not effaced, vain slaves of time. All beauty is imperishable, for it inscribes its reflection in the immortal light.

HELIBAH

What remains for us to ask of life on earth, then, except the decadence of our ecstasy? To await the threat of the enemy is to open one's flank to his blows. Amour only receives crowns from his sister, Death.

SARDANAPALUS

O terrestrial existence! It is not the garden of delights for which the insensates of the human herd seek. It cannot give its favorites happiness, nor the small change of joy. Only those who request suffering from it are wise. It cannot offer any other largesse. And since it has attributed to us the beauty of this hour, we shall quit it, grateful hearts. Death is summoning us with her superhuman voice.

HELIBAH

And we shall go enlaced through the door that she opens to us, the only one high enough for our heads exalted by kisses.

SARDANAPALUS

And since we are not attaining the sublime humility of accepting life, may our death cast over the earth a dazzling and durable light. Think, my beloved, for our supreme hymen, of the flamboyance of a kiss that the stars will perceive.

HELIBAH

Amorous couples who suffer on the earth, amorous couples enlaced on distant spheres, will you welcome with a smile of salutation the regal conflagration veiling the flames of our last kiss! Everything of us will be transformed, our flesh into ashes, our amour into a more profound union.

SARDANAPALUS

So be it!

(*The voices of the lovers vanish in the murmur of the kiss.*)

That night, the pastors scattered over the plain and the mountains, were astonished by a prodigious flamboyance dissipating the darkness. The breath of the wind carried away, with a swirl of sparks, the resinous odor of cedars and pines. The colossal light of the pyre rose toward the stars with the souls of the two lovers. It is still brooding beneath that ash, which is human memory: ash, the supreme adornment attributed to all pride.

THE MYSTERY OF AN INCARNATION

Et nunc et semper dilectae dicatum.[8]

In that epoch, in a vehement fit of misanthropy, I had retired to a grim bay on the Breton coast. The charm of a little village delightfully situated before the sea had arrested my footsteps of a voyager. The group of somber cottages where poor people lived with difficulty by fishing certainly had no special originality, but the soul of the location enveloped with mildness the saddened soul of the passer-by. Woods of oaks and elms isolated from the terrestrial horizon that cluster of huts, whose openings gaped toward that foliage, protected from the west wind by a rampart of abrupt granite ridges.

At that place, the landscape was divided into two antithetical parts. To the east, plunging into the earth, there was the joy of a dense and sumptuous vegetation; to the west, the ground entering as a promontory into the Atlantic consisted of a series of enormous granitic masses of a violent savagery. Camped in that village, I could contemplate simultaneously the two most contrary aspects of multiform nature: her most seductive smile and her most frightful convulsion.

Adjacent to the village, a very small cemetery descended in a gentle slope toward a strand forming a curt solution of continuity between the gaping cliffs of the coast. During high tides the flow came to brush the near-

---

[8] As it is now and ever shall be, hallowed beloved.

est graves. I shall never forget the impression that my first visit to that meager necropolis caused me. Enclosed in a wall at elbow height, one penetrated into it, as into almost all rural Breton cemeteries, by crossing a stile carved into the granite. An ardent sun made the blue sea shine. Tombstones festooned with brambles and ivy weighed upon the heavy yellow earth. Between them, old pines had grown, the thin bare trunks of which carried the rounded crowns high into the sky, opaque cods in which a few sparrows were chirping. Oh, the adorable cemetery! How delightfully the weary body would repose there, immortally lulled by the song of the waves. To the grandiose sepulcher of Chateaubriand on his solitary islet, I would have preferred a corner in that funerary field, where the angel of death must have smiled when he passed over it.

On the crosses I read Celtic names. A few inscriptions were analogous to this one: *To the memory of Jean-Yvon Guivarec'h, lost at sea.* Thus, several of the sepulchers cited the names of cadavers they had never received, which the waves still rolled on beds of pink algae. But those dead men, so the old men affirmed, came back every year to spend the day of the dead in the ordinarily empty tomb, in order to hear the prayers said for their soul by beloved voices.

One grave was florid with superb red roses, and had an aspect different from the others. It bore an ansate cross sculpted in the granite and charged with the following inscription:

MIRIAME HÉLÈNE
23 November ****-3 February ****
IRRADIAT HAEC ANIMA MEAM[9]

So the person whose remains repose there had only lived for two months! What unknowable destiny casts these beings into a world that they desert immediately? Something attracted me toward that sepulcher of a tiny infant. Why, in that cemetery of mariners, the strange mysticism of that Latin inscription? And was it by chance or not that the ansate cross displayed its form there, unusual in Christian countries and of which theologians, except perhaps for Tertullian, had not glimpsed the very ancient symbolism?[10]

Having returned to the inn, my first concern was to question the landlady about the tomb. There happened to be an old woman of the village there at that moment, old Katell, renowned in the surrounding area for speaking French admirably. Katell, glad to show off her talent as a storyteller to a "city monsieur," told me in her singsong voice a prolix tale from which I succeeded in disentangling the principal facts.

The little being asleep in the tomb for nearly fifty years had lived in an isolated house on the coast, a kilometer from the village. Once, someone who was then, according to Katell, a "young monsieur," had built that dwelling in order to come to it with his young wife and a little girl who had just been born.

---

[9] Irradiate this my soul.

[10] The "most ancient" symbolism of the ansate cross, or Egyptian ankh, is that of eternal life. More recently it symbolizes femininity; the astrological sign for the planet Venus is a version of it.

"Oh, Monsieur," Katell affirmed, "the beautiful child! But everyone said that she wouldn't live, because she was more beautiful than the angels of the good God. If you had seen her when she smiled! Oh, my God, for sure she heard the angels calling her!"

Of that child, whom she had perceived for a few moments nearly half a century ago, the old woman seemed to conserve an ever-present memory. I was not astonished by that, knowing the indestructible energy with which the memory of those simple folk retains the images it receives in the current of a monotonous life.

A few weeks after arriving, the child died.

"Monsieur," said Katell, "you're not going to believe me. Several times I've recounted the thing to painters passing through here, and I've seen that they took me for a old madwoman, All the same, it's necessary that I tell you. On the earth that covers the poor little body, the parents put armfuls of flowers; beautiful flowers, Monsieur, of a kind that never grow hereabouts. There were roses in the middle of February. They were roses flowered in hothouses, such as one sees in châteaux. Well, for more than a month, Monsieur, the roses stayed as fresh as the day they were picked. However, that winter, there were frosts and rain such as are hardly ever known. Six weeks later, there were still fresh flowers. They weren't new flowers, though, for no one in these parts would have been able to find roses in February, and the parents had gone to Paris. Ask Jean-Marie Elias, the gravedigger, whether I'm lying; he's very old but he still remembers everything I've told you there. And you, Charlotte," she added in Breton to the landlady, who was laying the table, "You're too young to have seen it, but your late mother must have told you about it."

"Ia," replied Charlotte, who did not speak French, "my mother often told me that my older brother, Lomic, who's navigating for the State at present was once very ill when he was very small. The doctor claimed that there was no more hope. My mother took Lomic to the little girl's tomb and said prayers, and my brother was cured in three days."

Candid souls, I thought, for whom all events conserve their aura of mystery; fortunate souls whose florescence has not been desiccated by the breath of sad cities and the evil century.

"But what became of the parents?" I asked Katell.

"The mother is dead, Monsieur. The father still lives in the house, of which you can see the roof from here. He lives there alone, served by the little girl's nurse, a foreigner from Paimpol, who hasn't ever quit her master since that time. Oh, the poor Monsieur, he was grief-stricken. Such a good man! There's never been an unfortunate in the neighborhood without the Monsieur having been good to him. In spite of that, people are a little afraid of him. He has such a funny way of looking at you. His house is full of books, which he spends his time reading, when he isn't walking along the coast."

"Has he been living like that for a long time?"

"Years and years, Monsieur. Once, when he was younger, he often went on voyages. Now, he no longer leaves the neighborhood."

During my lunch in the inn, Katell, while knitting, told me a host of anecdotes about the old man, trivial for the most part.

"This thing, Monsieur, my late husband could have told you if he were still in this world, poor dear. He'd been a leading seaman and could read like a priest. One day—oh, it was a long time ago—the Monsieur came to our house. 'Pierre,' he said to my man, would you care to take a glass of rum in the house? I have a favor to ask of you,'

"'I'm all yours, Monsieur,' my man replied. Oh, something funny had happened. Monsieur le Vicomte de X, the master of the Château de X, who was then a handsome fellow of twenty-two, had come to spend a few days in the neighborhood. He amused himself shooting the seagulls with his rifle all along the coast. The Monsieur liked the birds, and it caused him chagrin when anyone did them harm. He wrote the Vicomte a very nice letter to ask him not to shoot the seabirds any more. The Vicomte continued hunting them anyway. Then the Monsieur talked to him, and there was an argument.

"That was why the Monsieur came to look for my man. 'The Monsieur has asked me to be his witness,' Pierre said to me, when he came back. 'He's going to fight a duel with Monsieur le Vicomte.' My God! If it isn't frightful that men massacre one another like that! The two Messieurs fired pistol shots on the heath at Bizien, which you can see over there.

"The Vicomte fired first at the Monsieur without hitting him. The Monsieur said to him: 'Monsieur, I beg you, will you promise me not to kill the local birds any longer'

"'Monsieur," said the Vicomte, 'perhaps I'll reply when you've fired.'

"The Monsieur said to my man, who was further away than the Vicomte: 'Pierre, raise your hat the end of your arm and don't move!' And he fired into the hat, which was traversed by the bullet. Then the Vicomte held out his hand and said: 'Monsieur, I promise you to leave the birds that you love in peace.'"

Katell's verbiage, all the details that she gave me about the exterior life of the solitary, piqued my curiosity keenly.

In my walks along the coast I often encountered that singular individual. He was an agile and thin old man, whose face, framed by his white hair and beard, bronzed by the sun and sea breeze like those of mariners, was still handsome. The eyes, very young, shone with a moist gleam similar to one I had remarked in certain vegetarians or a few socialites habituated to injections of atropine.

I had certainly desired to make the acquaintance of the man, but he seemed little disposed to allow his grim solitude to be invaded, and sometimes he was unable to suppress a slightly hostile gaze directed at some passer-by whose silhouette importuned his reverie.

A fortunate circumstance obliged him to emerge from his reserve, and soon, a current of sympathy having linked us, I found myself admitted to the old man's intellectual intimacy. Having sealed his heart, he only opened it by a crack to his thought. I recognized quickly, by the power of his ideas, one of those men of genius, more numerous than one might believe, who, for one reason or another, disdain to work, and concentrate all their energies in the solitary expansion of their personality.

Recalled to Paris, I remained without news for a year of the old man whose magnificent intelligence had dazzled my youth. Then, one day, I received a package containing a manuscript and a letter thus conceived:

When you read these lines I will have quit the earth. I am bequeathing you the secret of the dolor that has tormented my life. A long time ago I swore to destroy the pages in which I was tempted to make this revelation. They are certainly unworthy of the being whose noble apparition they evoke. May they take wing in your hands! I have selected you as my confidant for reasons that you might not understand. Pardon me for speaking this. I have acquired the habit of divining in the present flower the future fruit, and I foresaw in your mind an efflorescence of which you might not have suspected the possibility yourself. You bear on your forehead the seal of the predestined who perceive the radiation of the Light. The last glimmers of my sunset salute your dawn.

I sought information. The old man had been found dead on his child's tomb one October evening.

As for the manuscript, I believe that I am deferring to its author's desire in publishing it in its integrity:

The Mystery of an Incarnation

I have often wondered, with anguish, whether I ought to recount the ineffable event that tore my life into two parts.

Ought I to bury in my heart, as in an inviolable tabernacle, the memory of the being who came to me from the depths of the Absolute? Ought I to deliver a description to the profane human herd, with a sacrilegious pen, of that divine emanation, whose disappearance I shall mourn forever?

As for what it makes of me, what does it matter? Whether, for having recounted with pious exactitude the story of a reality of which the observation surpasses their understanding, I might be treated as a liar, a visionary of a madman, I cannot bring myself to care. I am not accustomed to listen to the stammering of human ignorance. If others, more elevated in the spiritual hierarchy, attribute to me the charm of a deceptive imagination and the futile desire for a literary vainglory, their opinion cannot afflict my indifference.

But I hesitate to deliver to ignorant, vulgar or malevolent commentaries the sacred memory of a being whose mysterious advent could only be sensed by a few rare souls. Oh, frail child, little bird who perched for an hour on the tree of life, angel whose wing of light brushed my somber youth, advise me!

I believe that I discern the response:

"Always act for noble souls. Only think of the others in order to give them your pity. Even if there is only one just man or one genius on earth, think of that one, and remember that you owe him the revelation that you know. Speak: your voice will go toward the ears destined to hear it. When in the human crowd, a great soul cannot hold it in disdain. Every word of Truth of Beauty is a sun from which everyone can benefit in accordance with his ability; the eagle alone contemplates it, but the sparrow is warmed by its radiance. Speak. Why should you fear insult to the object of your worship? Blasphemy only injures those who proffer it Do you not know that the posthumous strength of martyrs increases in direct proportion to the maledictions launched but persecutors? What would the glory of saints be if evil did not exist? Speak!"

I am obeying.

In the course of my long existence, I have neglected the apparent action. Like all men whose intellect spreads its wings outside time, I could only accord a disdainful commiseration to the sterile agitation of Occidentals in my century. My life was uniquely sentimental and conceptual, and I only sent forth the falcon of my will to launch it into the gulf of the Mystery. For half a century, to the scorn of all minute mortals, only effort toward the Divine obsessed my thought.

In consequence of contingencies that it is superfluous to enumerate, my youth was much involved with society. In citing that detail, I desire to establish that I was not a contemplative hermit whose vision was deformed by solitude. At twenty-five years of age it was given to me to acquire an experience of men capable of challenging that of those miserable old men who take pleasure in the vanity of social intrigue for long years.

I was twenty-six when the event that determined my subsequent life occurred: my wife became pregnant.

Hélène was then twenty-three. She recalled that type of Virgin that certain northern Primitives, like Memling and Jan Van Eyck cherished. The law of attractions had pushed us toward one another; but her mind, although moving under its native impulsion in the sphere of ideas into which I launched myself, conserved its originality while blossoming in contact with mine. It was certainly impregnated by the emanations of my thought, but without losing the charm of its initial perfume. Her profound soul, a marvelous keyboard with which the fingers of angels, playing thereon, awoke harmonious intuitions, was revealed in her candid dark eyes and in the archaic quality of her beauty, attesting the phenomenon of heredity called by modern physiologists "atavism," thanks to which a being resembles some ascendant, a prototype of its race. But the aggressive energy of the ancestor, a warrior of the Renaissance, a famous Maréchal de France whose family had possessed the crown of Bretagne in distant centuries, was transformed in the young woman into a force of melancholy gentleness.

At the certainty of her maternity, Hélène was gripped by an anxiety that I shared. To summon a soul to life from the depths of the Unknown was a responsibility that our youth did not envisage without trembling.

"So be it," affirmed the young mother. "This child will be my masterpiece. Intoxicated by the Beautiful, my spirit is a bird that flies among worlds from which it returns dazzled, without being able to bring back the smallest flower in its rosy beak as testimony. If I were a man I would be subject to the torture of poets impotent to realize their vision. The faculty of expression was refused me, and sometimes I was saddened to sense myself artistically sterile. Yes, this child will be my masterpiece. I want to create a sublime being, a being of Light and Beauty. And the ideal I glimpse behind a veil of mist, he will contemplate with his eagle eyes, in an integral splendor, with the serene limpidity of genius."

From then on, it was agreed that we would unite our forces in order to awaken to life a magnificent human model.

"But it is not today that that work is commencing," I said to Hélène. "Every effort of elevation, every minute of exaltation toward the Divine pierced under one of its multiple manifestations, every beat of the wing toward the triangle of the Beautiful, the True and the Just, every one of the vanished volitions that constitute the noble part of our past: all that is not lost, any more than the burden of our weaknesses and errors. And it is because you are natally pure that it will be permitted to you to give birth to a superior being.

Hélène delivered herself entirely to her work of creation, with a constant energy, scrupulously following my successive indications.

Of that arrival of a child in the terrestrial world, the mystery of incarnation that disconcerts humans, I could only reveal certain phases to her, but her marvelous intuition penetrated at a stroke arcana on which the meditation of admirable thinkers has labored for a long time.

By means of the enlightenment drawn from my studies I was able to lift some of the veils by which the secret of the Word made flesh is enveloped by modern science, which only knows the modifications of the phenomena of embryology, and by religions, all of which, in the symbolism of the Fall and the Redemption, inform those who can understand of a part of the eternal Truth.

Exoteric science, on the physical plane to which its investigation its limited, has glimpsed, albeit very incompletely, under the name of Evolution, one of the primordial laws that order the world. It has not yet understood that the Law in question is mystically enunciated under the title of Redemption, by all theologies. But it does not know, and doubtless never will know, at the opposite pole, the law of Involution that religions call the Fall, in accordance with which births are operated.

How does a soul, an emanation of the Absolute descending the spiral of Involution, enter into matter? How it is borne away by the vertigo of the Fall, toward the womb of a woman, the first human tomb? Of that mystery, I can only lift a little of the veil here.

By way of Amour, by means of the august embrace of their flesh, the human couple attaches to a parcel of matter a principle of Universal Life. Thus is created a center of attraction, the power of which radiates toward the spheres in which spirits desirous of incarnation circulate. The Word of a couple summons a soul of their race. The higher it launches toward the zenith of Infinity, the more beautiful and more noble is the one that responds to the carnal invitation. But it can happen that the wing of Amour occasionally carries the generative virtuality of a vulgar couple beyond their sphere of customary attraction, and that is why a beautiful woman or a pure genius is sometimes born to a bourgeois couple magnified for an instant by the ecstasy of a spasm.

Like everything else in the world, spirits waiting to put on a corporeal form obey the law of Hierarchy. It is an elementary spirit that enters into the skin of a boor; it is a spirit already florid by virtue of an anterior development that will inhabit the brain of a Dante. "Everything created is a revelation in the Flesh," say all the mystics via the voice of Novalis. And the highest revelation is incarnate in Heroes, the supreme types of humanity that pious Hellas once proclaimed demigods: Phidias, Shakespeare, Leonardo da Vinci, Plato, Saint John, Jacob Boehme..."

"I want to be the mother of a child of that beauty," Hélène sad.

"Be careful! Every grandeur is expiated by a dolor. Seven swords are reserved for the hearts of glorious mothers."

"Often, alas, those of humble mothers too. Popular belief affirms that during pregnancy, the sentiments of the mother influence the child."

"It is right. The popular soul is the well in which the pure water of Truth is stagnant. Ancient Greece knew an art unknown to moderns, those contemplators of Beauty: callipedia, the art of creating beautiful children."

"Can you reconstitute that art, friend?"

"We can try."

"But first it would be necessary to know the sex of the child."

"That is easy. We can determine it by either of two procedures: that of contemporary physiologists or that of the ancient sages. In the meantime, we can have recourse to magnetic lucidity. All forms are inscribed, outside time, in the sidereal light, as in a succession of instantaneous photographic prints. A magnetized human whose sidereal body is put in communication with that universal receptacle of reflections perceives those forms, inaccessible to anyone who is not in a state of Vision."

I put a young woman to sleep, whose lucidity I had previously proven.

"It's a girl," she said. "Oh, how beautiful she is! She will be born in the first fortnight of December, on a Saturday, before midnight. It's impossible for me to read the exact date, or to know any more. Wake me up."

The sex being known, it was necessary to give the child a name.

To name a being is to consecrate it, to dress it in a cope of silk or a shirt of Nessus; it is to attach a talisman of gold or lead to its neck. Certainly, nothing is indifferent to human destiny, and the eventualities that the vulgar attribute to absurd chance are manifest as the effects of unknown causes. But the will that associates the individuality of a being with the sonority of a few syllables is making an unconscious incantation, the vibrations of which, refracted by the shield of Destiny, fall back upon the head of the living being in waves of curses or glory, sadness or felicity. On that truth, the divination of great poets habituated to manipulating the evocative virtue of words is in accord with the science of the Prophets. It is said in the Vedas: "You shall give your daughter a sonorous name, abundant in vowels and soft in fluttering on human lips." Around the cradles of legendary princes, godmother fays invested the frail godsons with fortunate syllables, and it is not in futility that religions baptize newborns with the already illustrious names of martyrs or saints, beings of a superior humanity that surround the subsequent veneration of races with an occult force.

The child received the names Miriame Hélène, each expressing the feminine ideal of a civilization.

The Hebraic vocable Miriame, the hieroglyphic mystery of which I shall not explain here, designated the woman whose forehead is crowned with the seven stars and whose feet trample the serpent of astral light.

In the Homeric myth, Hélène, the woman whose charming wake the Trojan old men followed ecstatically, bears a name that, preceded by a new hierogram, is attached to the light of the moon—Selene—and of which the root El recalls "immutable," in the initial languages of the Orient, the residues of the mother tongue, the whole concept of splendor, glory and magnificence. If it is for rare seers that the name Hélène awakes the metaphysical revelation contained in its suave sonority, thanks at least to a long tradition, it represents to a greater number of less profound imaginations the idea of supreme beauty, the most radiant form of humanity that nature has caused to spring from her womb.

A name contains within it a representation of the ensemble of thoughts whose correspondences it summons in the person who pronounces it. It therefore combines with its essential virtue that which is attributed to it by the tradition of a human collectivity, and that by which it is magnetized by the will that cloaks a being therewith. A name is a living symbol of the being that it designates.

Bearing in her loins an unknown being, which her maternity was summoning from the heart of the Infinite,

Hélène considered herself as a temple that ought not to be profaned by any vile thought or vision of ugliness.

"Spirit of my child, so long as your obscure form fills my womb, you shall live in me as in a splendid palace, in which the genius of great artists has painted the walls with frescoes. I shall never think of you, or any part of you, without associating with it some idea of beauty…but," she asked me, "has the soul of a child entered into it while the mother bears it?"

"According to the secret doctrine, the soul only commences to attach itself to the fetus when it has a brain—which is to say, in accordance with the evidence of embryology, toward the eighth month; but it floats around it then. It is only at the moment of birth that it penetrates it, at the same time as the fist breath of air, just as, at death, it is exhaled with the last breath. In any case, the essential soul is never allied as narrowly with the body as certain theologians teach exoterically. Irreducible to carnal imprisonment, it is the aura in which form bathes. Your soul is your ideal."

The people who appeared, an adorable missionary, to give our world the most magnificent revelation of beauty, the Greeks, installed noble works of art in the dwellings of women in order that the eyes of mothers, haunted by perpetual images of beauty, might imagine sons as charming as the gods. Like those genitrices, Hélène surrounded herself with an atmosphere of beauty. Living in Paris during the period of her gestation, she spent whole days in the Louvre.

The moderns do not comprehend the harmony of the human body. How can a race habituated to consider nudity as shameful understand the marvelous poem of plasticity? That sacrilegious ignorance of her most admirable masterpiece, just nature chastises in the very flesh of those brutal hypocrites. She fashions them with grotesque torsos, filthy belies and hideous limbs and launches them into the irony of light, heaps of amorphous meat, in order that one day, some vengeful power, some grim Daumier will whip their ignominious appearance immortally.

Triumphing over time, Greek statuary insults them with its glory and transports with pure joys the human elite, ever renewed, to whom destiny assigns the mission of conserving the flame of the altar of divine Beauty.

Of the Hellenic masterpieces, the one that inspired the most intense emotion in Hélène, the one that twisted all her fibers with a frisson and covered her young face with the sacred pallor that adolescent poets give to a fine verse, was the Victory of Samothrace. Oh, a curse upon the cause that mutilated that sublime body! Certainly, the great hand that sculpted you in marble, O Victory, petrified soul, did not want to make you the monstrous allegory of the massacre of one army by another, the apotheosis of murder and brutality. O august form, I know the desire with which your feet vibrate on your stone rostrum. You are the victory of humanity over Hell, the triumph of the Triangle on high over the Triangle below, of truth over error, of good over evil, of beauty over ugliness; and the lyrical thrust of your loins, the impetuous flight of your large wings, bear you straight toward the climate of your homeland, toward the mystery of your dream, toward the bosom of the divine.

Like all artists loving the spiritualized character of form, Hélène reproached the normal body of woman for the heaviness of the thighs, twin columns supporting the excessively powerful entablature of the pelvis and the rump, a massive architecture whose weight crushes the frail stems of the ankles. Thus the female appears a su-

93

perb animal of reproduction, all of whose energies are concentrated in the abdomen, a vast temple of fecundity. Veiling that fault, the author of the Venus Victrix was obliged to surround with drapery the legs and the raised knee, in order to cause the flower of the adorable torso to spring forth from the isoperimetric shaft.

The young mother evoked on the horizon of her imagination a slimmer ideal of feminine plasticity, ennobled by the virile elegance of the adolescent, close to that attempted by the sculptors of Hermaphrodites extended in the Louvre on their marble cushions.

Day by day, she populated the memory of her pupils with the most radiant heads that the hands of great masters had caressed. The Virgins of the Italian Primitives, the tapering ovals of those faces ever feature of which reveals and energy of tenderness and amour, the serene candor of those gilded foreheads, had invades her vision like beloved portraits. It was to those types of feminine beauty, scantly various, that her mind consecrated its sisterly kiss: to the women of Florentines and Umbrians, those whose voluptuous melancholy Sandro Botticelli adored and those whose pink cheeks Perugini animated with a pagan joy of living. But above all, a magnetic attraction drew Hélène to the women of the supreme hero of painting, the divine Leonardo da Vinci. How she absorbed the profound grace and the enigmatic softness of those profiles, which smiled in knowing the arcana of death and life.

Among those creatures of beauty, had she chosen a prototype after which her voluntary thought attempted to model in her entrails the face of her child? She remembers that one day, in the Academy of Florence, before the archangel soaring with sword in hand in Botticelli's *Tobias*, she had exclaimed in a surge of passionate admiration: "Of, if I had a son, I would like him to resemble him!"

I found a reproduction of the head of the archangel: dense dark curls framing the purity of the outline of genius, enlivening the warm dullness of an even complexion in which an intrinsic ardor is affirmed, directed by will; eyes of a tranquil heroism, a mouth born for the voluptuous kiss of ides; the face of a being capable of putting his dream into action after having conquered it in a superhuman domain. Gentle as it might be, that face is male; Hélène feminized it in her imagination. It was on that flower of archangelic humanity that the butterfly of her dream alighted most frequently. But, an artist without a work, she preferred above all the personal idea of beauty that surged forth in the solitary intimacy of her vision, and which she wanted to realize in flesh.

Every form reveals a soul. To influence the form of a living being, it is first necessary to influence its soul. Hélène extended toward her daughter's soul her thought charged with the genius of great poets and divinatory music. She plunged recklessly into the dream of the highest minds. Celtic in origin, she disdained the mediocrity of the French genius, which, until the dawn of the nineteenth century, had not been able to give the world a single great poet. Shakespeare, Dante and the French Romantics reigned over her ambiance, but above all, she lingered over lyric poets whose dream quivered with an occult vertigo, the chaste ideal of which launched forth like a golden lily from a gulf of shadow, the amour of which flew toward women of angelic essence, such as Edgar Poe and Charles Baudelaire. Around her, companions evoked by her election, matched the likes of Leonore, Ligeia, Poe's Morella, Balzac's Séraphita,

Shelley's Queen Mab, all heroines over which fell the influx of the Moon, the dispenser of melancholy.

That exaltation, which the young woman drank like a sacred wine, those spiritual forces with which she armed her imagination, it was necessary to concentrate toward the unique goal; it was necessary to constrain them to envelop the soul of the child with a sphere of sumptuous ideality. What talisman would have the power of the Flamboyant Star of the magical Pentagram?

The moderns are unaware of the virtue of Signs. They do not know that every symbol contains, living and multiplied, the idea that it represents, and by virtue of the energy of which it can act on nature. Will they ever understand that a man can charge a Sign with the fluid of his will?

Hélène often absorbed herself in the contemplation of the invigorating sign. Everywhere, the design of the Star with five points shone before her thought, which she guided toward the future form of the child as, in occult legend, it guided the three Oriental Magi toward the child of Bethlehem.

A honey-bee of sublimity, Hélène had taken pollen from the purest flowers of human genius. If she thought of some feature of the face that she wanted her daughter to have, she immediately summoned to the mirror of her imagination the special beauty of that feature. For example, if she thought about the eyes, she visualized them, while singing in her memory, a sonorous accompaniment of a realized Word, these profound lines:

Large eyes of my child, adored arcana,
You greatly resemble the magical grottoes
In which, behind the mass of lethargic shadows
Unknown treasures scintillate vaguely.

We decided to place our efforts under the invocation of an intercessor of the elite among the great masters of the Word, among the mild heroes that follow, charmed, the man, the lion, the eagle and the bull. The soul of that dead man, faithful to our appeal, was to watch over our work and caress with his breath the forehead of our child.

Our choice settled on Apollonius of Tyana. The great pagan Mage is alive in a glory that has not been profaned by the vulgar. Only initiates venerate his memory, which has not been sullied by the mud of universal renown. Obscure messiah, no human infamy has been committed in your pure immortal name. In the empyrean of Prophets, where you are enthroned in the presence of your sacred brethren, next to Gautama the Buddha and Mohammed, beneath Jesus Christ, your side does not bleed like theirs, and your serenity laments for them and consoles them. For the truth and justice that their generous hands attempted to bring to humans, humans transmuted into lies and iniquity. Their divine names decorate social ignominy, and that is why, Apollonius, son of God, I preferred you to your sacred brothers.

Miriame appeared in the world on the second Saturday in December,[11] as the seer had announced.

To anyone who can penetrate the mystery of forms, every infant reveals the being that she will be in the maturity of her development. No more than an adult, a newborn cannot conceal the soul inscribed in her flesh.

---

[11] This conflicts with the date recorded on the tombstone, as reported earlier in the story.

If Hélène and I had been alone in observing the strange beauty of our child, I certainly would not insist upon it, anxious of perhaps having seen it with the partiality of a father; but no stranger, however indifferent they might be to the prestige of the ideal, passed close to her without attesting an admiration, as if some secret force emanating from that tiny body had constrained those passers-by to rise toward a domain higher than their habitual thoughts.

In contemplating her daughter, Hélène was swelled by the triumphant joy of creators. She had in her exactly what she had wanted. She had wrought her ideal; she had realized it in life; and that masterpiece was a being that deployed a soul—everything proved it!—a great human soul, one of those that participate most directly in the divine soul.

Certainly, I have never seen, neither among the living nor among the figure summoned to the virtual existence of works of art, a creature as beautiful as Miriame was a month after her birth. Each of her features had a very emphatic individuality, and yet the ensemble was not marked by the aged character that generally devolves to newborns whose face is less imprecise than usual.

An unusual profundity of feminine beauty, and a charm of masculine gentleness, enveloped that forehead, whose admirable contours announced the rare harmony of equilibrated powers. The artistic type with which Miriame's profile presented the greatest resemblance was the feminine type dear to Leonardo da Vinci, but the child's expression was more superhuman.

A nocturnal splendor emanated from that mat flesh with golden reflections, helmed with thick raven-black hair. The oval was elongated with an elegance that even Van Dyck never knew. One would have searched in vain for an imperfection in any of her features. The dark crimson mouth was designed so purely that it seemed affianced to the kiss of a god; the nose, proudly modeled, revealed a desire of suave authority; the eyes, the large eyes, under the charming arches of the eyebrows, were hollowed out in a vast double abyss of darkness sometimes illuminated by a golden scintillation.

Miriame was one month old when we decided to come and live in our house in Bretagne, in order to bring up the little Parisienne in the best conditions. The wives of the mariners, rude and fecund Breton women, were fascinated by the child, and their naïve ecstasy, their religious admiration and their candid intuition in contemplating in her a mysterious being, astonished me. In the function of her sidereal respiration, every human individual emits an aura, a magnetic atmosphere only perceptible by virtue of its effects, at least to those who have not developed in themselves the faculty of sight that Paracelsus named the sixth sense. Miriame was thus enveloped by an extraordinary power of attraction and beneficent domination.

The strange precocity of the child alarmed me. Perhaps I will be charged with hallucination; what does it matter? In accordance with the methods of my times, in brushing all levels of Parisian society, I had developed a habit of analytical observation whose mechanical function could not be troubled by the most intense emotion; and the testimony of everyone who saw our child corroborates my own.

I remember one improbable event. Miriame was then awakening to the sixth day of her existence. She was reposing in a crib adjacent to her mother's bed. Like all newborns, she sometimes made nervous grimaces in which maternal illusion salutes joyfully the first manifestation of consciousness; but this time—no error was possible—it was not a grimace. It was what popular language, always so accurately imagistic, calls an angelic smile. The child's entire face brightened; a smile so ecstatic, so unfathomable passed over her mouth and her eyes that Hélène, her heart suddenly traversed by a sibylline anguish, uttered a vehement cry, a visceral cry, as if to recall that frail adventurous soul from an unknown world.

A month later, when her mother took her in her arms, the grateful child saluted her creator with that smile, attenuated by a serene expression of humanity; and, extending toward her the inaugural beauty of her hands, she exclaimed, in a painful effort toward speech.

Then suffering fell upon that light prey. A pneumonia and a gastritis combined to torture her. Oh, I always have in my heart that pale dolorous head, that long emaciated oval and the somber lairs of the eyes, radiant, under the crepe of the lashes, with the muted majesty of martyrdom. Oh, little soul of my desperate amour, why did you suffer so much? What is the good of my vain science, which could not protect you?

For three days it was necessary to await the end. It was seven o'clock in the morning, on a Thursday in February—the slightest details of that day will live in me forever—as the moon set. Miriame, at the utmost degree of weakness, was touched by the wing of death. Oh, we sensed her soul escaping from her lips. In vain I had attempted the theurgical miracle. It was the supreme moment.

Then Hélène, in the paroxysm of human dolor, seizing her daughter's hands, uttered an appeal of strange power: "Miriame!" How the sonority of that cry still quivers in my ear! The dying chills—oh, dead already—

opened her eyes. An ineffable expression passed into that gaze. And life returned in her as in the daughter of Jairus at the voice of the Master of Galilee. The two little hands clasped the mother's thumbs with all the force of their weakness, in order to draw vitality therefrom. And if Hélène attempted a gesture, a withdrawal of her hands, the infant clung to the thumbs with an unexpected energy, at the same time as her eyes, oh, those eyes of prayer and amour...

From seven o'clock in the morning until three o'clock in the afternoon, Hélène remained inclined over the crib without interruption, her thumbs in her daughter's hands, imposing on that tender agonizing body the magnetism of vitality. She was there, insensible, isolated from the world, all the forces of her being extended toward an invincible will: the salvation of her child. And beside her, my will corroborated hers.

At about four o'clock, the physician arrived. He had not hurried, certain that he would find death in the house. He inspected the child with amazement.

"She's saved!" he cried. "Nature sometimes works miracles, but this one, I cannot even seek to understand."

How could he have understood, a poor brain uniquely filled with a meager scholarly science and a few personal observations, that love is stronger than death, and that Hélène's had recalled the animating principles to the dying, to the dead? An intuitive thaumaturge, the desperate mother had triumphantly manipulated the mysterious virtue of the voice and the transmission of vital force via the fingers and the eyes.

Miriame recovered her health. Hope sang within us, but the wings of misfortune were hovering, wide open. Abruptly, three days later—it was exactly seven o'clock in the morning, on Sunday, as the moon set—the child died.

For three days and three nights I did not quit the crib where the dear little body lay among the roses. The serenity of death had effaced the memory of the death-throes from the pale mask. How beautiful she was, thus, in inviolable immobility! Oh, so sadly beautiful! I shall see her eternally, that waxen head with the pale gold reflection, and the vast profundity of the eyes that I did not want to close, and the mouth, the adorable mouth in which that proud color of dark crimson was still resplendent. If you had grown up, O superhuman creature, if the earth had seen you as a woman, what man would have been worthy of your amour? You ought to have been the bride of a god.

Of that mysterious being, one inexplicable detail will trouble me forever. We had wanted her admirable form to be surrounded by flowers. Flowers, those existences of beauty, innocence and perfume, were the only objects in this world meriting the caress of her hands. In order to fortify that vanished soul with the virtue of a sign, Hélène had wanted to make her a cross of flowers herself. To two equal arms, disposed in the form of a Greek cross, her fingers attached roses, hyacinths and viburnum; in the center she put an enormous tea-rose, for the occult symbolism of the Rose and the Cross.

When, in a harsh February frost, the last spadeful of earth had fallen lugubriously on the little body, the flowery cross was laid on top of armfuls of flowers at the place in the cemetery that has since become so familiar to my knees. Six weeks later, outside the heap of rotten flowers, the tea-rose at the center of the cross still surged forth as fresh as if it were blooming on the bush. Frost, rain and the torments had passed over tits petals without withering them. How? Why? That strange phenomenon was repeated several times. The following winter, chrysanthemums remained on the grave for two months without withering.

From you, sweet creature of superhumanity, therefore, such a powerful virtue emanated, such a profound beneficence, that your proximity alone embalmed with a vital energy the chrysanthemums and the roses, flowers as beautiful as you, and like you, so short-lived. Since you charmed the angel of death in their favor, oh, why did you let him carry you away in his arms?

Miriame was born in a year ruled by the Moon, on the fourth day of the new moon. She died, after two synodic months, on the fourth day of the new moon. Several times I had observed a malign selenic influence upon her. And long calculation, later, provided revelations...

How many time I have cursed destiny! Daughter of my flesh and my thought, why, then, did you come to earth to fly away so rapidly? The mystical belief of the ancient initiates is true: those who die young are beloved by the gods. The solitary seer of Scandinavia is right: there are souls so pure that for them, the duration of the terrestrial proof in limited to a few days. They only brush the earth; they cannot become entangled with it. They rise again, with an immediate thrust, into the involutive spiral that leads to the increate light, toward the divine entelechy. As soon as they Fall, they soar to Redemption.

However, I revolted. My flesh cried out toward your presence, my child. I have not enjoyed seeing you, I have not seen you in the harmonic development of your strength and your grace. Your mysterious power, which your infantile form revealed, I anticipated without ever seeing it blossom in the triumphant youth of a woman. I had penetrated the soul of your beauty so deeply! What did you bring in your beautiful hands of a prophetess? Perhaps the blessings of a redeemer, such as infinity delegates to humankind from time to time. You might have consoled the exile of noble souls. Poor humanity, it will always be unaware of the loss it suffered in you. In any case, has it ever understood such losses? When Shakespeare died, how many wept? At Golgotha, how many wept for Jesus? Who, then, except for me, could remember your aborted grandeur, the grandeur manifested to me alone?

A torment has haunted me for a long time. Was your death my punishment? Was I temeritous in wanting to manipulate the redoubtable forces of the Word, wanting, as a man, to create like a God? At any rate, I have suffered the torture of Prometheus. On your tombstone, my daughter, to which my loins are riveted, the vulture of regret has lacerated my liver.

In life, I sense your soul illuminating mine with an interior radiation. *Irradiat haec anima meam.* And I await the hour of exit when you will come to fetch me for the mystery of Becoming, the hour when your hands, your beautiful hands of theophany, with a tutelary gesture, will open the supreme Golden Door to the soul of your father.

AMONG ALL GAZES

To Ennemond Faye[12]

Are you a prince among Sages? Have you been able to become the majestic solitary individual whose luminous will shelters him from the respiration of the crowd? Have you forged, for your bosom steeped seven times in the Absolute, the adamantine armor against which the daggers of destiny break? Do you remain devoid of weakness, faithful to the quadruple oath of being able to abstain, to suffer, to die and to forgive? If you have marched so far on the superhuman path, Master, I salute you; intercede in the Invisible for your belated brother!

For my life is not yet liberated from ambient influences. The effluvia of beings, living, dead or virtual, assail my breast with their authority. Sometimes I have sensed their tenacious virtue in gazes cast toward my shadow. Yes, by means of the eyes, above all, those dehiscences of his most real power, a man shines upon the destiny of his neighbor. The people, instinctive guardians, watching over the treasure of the most profound notions, express their trouble in gazes of hatred. "Oh, if those eyes were pistols, I'd not longer be standing!" Certain pupils of conscious jettaturas can launch death like those of the basilisk and catoblepas. Passer-

---

[12] Unlike most of the dedicatees of Michelet's stories, Ennemond Faye (1862-1913) was not a writer but a businessman who promoted tram systems in several cities in the Midi.

by, you receive a sideways glance without peril if your heart is pure or your soul is valiant. Reverberated, it will strike its author more murderously. Do you think that gazes of tenderness or amour have not tamed death? If you are coming from the arms of a sincere lover, you can run disdainfully toward the menace of swords, for the gaze that her soul exhaled toward you, at the moment of your departure, armors you efficaciously.

Among all the gazes that meet me, I still see several whose temporary projection enveloped my bosom with a permanent net. Sometimes, on the road where I am accomplishing the pilgrimage of the tomb, I am enabled to sense around me the presence of one of those vivacious gazes of old. Apparently, the beings who poured from their pupils in that fashion a respiration of their souls only brushed my life as casual passers-by. No contact, no speech, links them to my memory.

They were women whose kiss I did not know, men who hands I have not shaken or whose swords I have not parried, children whose preordained foreheads I have not caressed, surge forth from a corner of my route and disappear. Doubtless I shall not encounter them again. And yet, at certain moments of annoying lucidity, their memory rises in my mind like morning mist in a meadow. Gazes of passers-by, you have the melancholy attraction of destinies without accomplishment...

Certainly, that evening, I had no intention of going to the Opéra ball. A succession of incidents brought me to pass in front of the monument at about one o'clock in the morning, in a dinner jacket. Was it the joyful rush toward the doors of sparkling dominos or the gracious chatter of shrill feminine voices behind the masks that induced me to go in? I have not identified the obscure force that advised me at the time.

For half an hour I wandered through the ball without anything having penetrated me from that drunken multitude. The joy of crowds ordinarily acts upon the individual in one of two different and opposite ways. Either it submerges his personality and rolls it in its powerful waves as a river in flood ferries wreckage, or, if it encounters a seed of sadness in him, it develops it by means of a force of reaction, with the result that a man never emerges from a crowd without carrying away either the interior echo of an excitement, if he has abandoned himself to the collective sentiment, or, if he has resisted it, a durable depression. That evening, however, I did not feel, between my solitary soul and that of the delirious crowd, either a communion or a contest.

It seemed that a mysterious sword had traced a magic circle around my feet uncrossable by exterior influences. Only my eyes rejoiced in the dazzling aspect of the scene, although it was made to seduce a young man whom no imperious passion wounded. In the hall, I had followed for a long time, through the atmosphere gilded by disk, the sparkling tournament of costumes, embellished by the enchantment of the lighting.

It amused me to see, on the florid balconies of the boxes, pretty feminine silhouettes offering to desires, beneath the lace of a mask, the expansion of their cleavages, their breasts surging from the bodice in the ardor of the moment, and their naked arms bombarding black coats with bunches of violets, hyacinths and camellias, which riposted smiling.

At the exit from the foyer, where the rustling queue of bright dominoes flowed with the grace of a marvelous serpent, cutting through the air, heavy with breath and perfumes, with merry screeches and laughter muffled by satin-lined hoods or mantillas, I went to lean on one of the corbelled balustrades that overlooked the celebrated staircase. I had only been there for a moment when the sentiment of a presence close by obliged me to turn round.

Then I perceived, rising within me, the pallor that death and great commotions of amour cause. A young woman was there, whose gaze had summoned mine mysteriously, and we both lived a minute of extraordinary life.

While the couple who accompanied her at the masked ball—a sister, I thought, for the two women resembled one another in attitudes and costume, and a gracious young man—leaned over the balustrade to watch the sprightly ascent of arrivals, she held back a little, prey to the unknown force that linked us together by the beam of our gazes. Under the Bruges mantilla that veiled her face rigorously, leaving nothing uncovered, like the Muslims, except her somber eyes, from which fire seemed to spring, I divined her own pallor, and the oppressed movement of her breasts. Later, I reconstituted all the details of her person, which were perhaps penetrated then by a duplicated fraction of my mind, for as long as her apparition lasted, I was uniquely possessed by her.

Her cream satin dress, while accompanying the supple beauty of her body with an elegance, did not constitute, with the accessories of her costume, the perfectly harmonious ensemble that reveals the supreme Parisienne. Certain notes in the arrangement, excluding the eccentricity devoid of tradition of the foreigner and the redundancy of the provincial, indicated the classic and timorous elegance of the Parisienne of the left bank.

In any case, in that solemn minute, nothing of that woman was hidden from me. The abnormal glimmer of her eyes illuminated for me all the darkness of her life before the indifferent. Through the lace, the slender oval of her face appeared to me, as her noble body did through the fabrics, as a solitary passes his heart through the veils of time: a moment of plenitude in which our two individualities were fused as harmoniously as in the surge of the most intimate embrace.

"Are you coming?" her companion, thus far attentive to the entrance of the fête, said to the young woman.

And the one who had opened to me the horizon of her gaze passed her arm beneath that of her sister, and departed with the gracious couple. I took a step to follow in her tracks—for were we not linked forever?—and she turned toward me, but the speech of her eyes stopped me,

"Don't come!" sang her profound pupils. "You must not. What joy of kisses could equal the intensity of the moment we have just lived? The orbits of our two destinies intersected at the unique point in space and time that was assigned to them. Neither you nor I will ever forget that moment. We will carry the secret charm in an indelible envelope. Let us each go toward our end. To other men, my loins will devolve; other women will shiver in your arms. Accept me for what I am: the annunciatrix of the promise of amour."

I allowed her to disappear.

I arrived, at the nascent dawn, in the old Spanish town, a feudal sentinel of pink granite raising its marvelous archaic silhouette on the edge of the ocean. Scarcely had I dismounted from my bicycle in order to climb the steep street that led to the medieval tower than the powerful architectures had penetrated me with their occult spirits.

In the morning and evening twilights, towns, before their awakening or their slumber, meditate in a more profound consciousness of their own life. At those hours, when their diurnal grace or their nocturnal beauty is about to become precise, while the aromas rise more forcefully from their surrounding countryside, cities respire their mysterious breath more abundantly. The solitary and concentrated soul of that Spanish citadel took possession of its guest of a morning.

Its grim history, of which I had been unaware as I crossed the threshold of the postern, imposed itself on my memory with an increasing authority. The absolute harmony of that rude nature, those men and that human endeavor, had effaced all distance between the ancient town and the passing stranger. That fortress perched like an age's nest between the mountains and the sea, poured into me violently the intuition of its tragic past, and persuaded me that I had lived for a long time in the narrow circle of its ramparts, amid its august memories, against the friction of its inhabitants with closed faces. And, alone in the auroral silence, the guttural chant of a little rope-maker unwinding his wheel at the foot of the enclosing wall seemed to me to be a familiar song.

A series of violent impressions was reserved for me in that corner of the earth. At the summit of the tower I had received the emotion of a solemn beauty: an impetuous kiss of the ocean to the mountain under the benediction of the roseate sky, before the taciturn crown of the ancient town. Then, in the courtyard of the ruined castle, between the high fuliginous walls, a secular odor of crimes, tortures and lust oppressed my breast, and the heavy and certain breath of very ancient phantoms weighed upon my shoulder. The revived evocation of ferocious amours and the indestructible memory of blood gripped me. I found myself outside with a sigh of relief.

In the *calle mayor*, women were going down toward the church for a mass in commemoration of a dead man. Their slow and grave silhouettes, of which the face alone protruded from the uniform black veil falling from the cranium to the kidneys, glided along the walls with the majesty of antique bas-reliefs. I entered behind them into the church overloaded with shadows, light and gilt, a tenebrous temple stared by candle flames and golden flowers, stifling, like a vast tomb in which the convulsions of vehement amours and desperate sensualities vibrated beyond death. Toward what tragic and jealous god did prayers fly here?

The black troop of women were praying, kneeling down, with a placidity revealing the fact that death, the companion of ancient lusts, created an atmosphere agreeable to their bosoms. Next to each one, a long twisted candle burned at both ends, illuminating their curbed black backs with russet gleams

At the exit from that somber mass, a young woman in hooded mourning-dress, who was walking in front of me, turned round on the parvis to offer me holy water. The brief friction of our fingers stirred us with a frisson. An accumulation of anterior desires with which we were both charged encountered its fulgurant expansion. Via our intersecting gazes, the magnetic exchange ran through our immobilized bodies.

She was not twenty years old, that ardent daughter of ancient races, but the passions emanating from that sky, that soil and that town, magnetized her voluptuous beauty. I remember her heavy pupils, bronzed like those warm nights that carry around the world the pollen of flowers and pubescent sighs. Certainly, that was not the banal appeal of a beautiful girl to fleeting desire. The charm that she radiated led to the threshold of the alliance of lust and death, and the kiss of her arched mouth, a bright flower in the mat flesh, evoked disastrous joys.

Why did the gaze of that young woman, among all others, translate to me with such force the twin mystery of amour and death? It was not chance. Like those of the elements, the encounters of beings are irrevocable.

The schooner glided in the grip of the gentle breeze that sustained its canvas so lightly, outside everything, that the hull almost furrowed, almost without pitching, the abrupt waves murmuring in the night. For several hours we had been skirting the coast in order to admire its languid grace in the moonlight. Leaning over the side, I gazed at the Mediterranean panorama. The terrain, staged in very precise planes in the stellar light, rose slowly toward the distant horizon, covered here and there by broad sheets of somber vegetation. Then, at intervals, overflowing toward the shore, villages of fishermen, of small houses, the vivid Italian colors of which flourished vaguely in the silvery light: a beautiful landscape of peace, silence and security.

"Oh!" pronounced a woman's voice on the deck. "Oh, captain, land there!"

That pretty caprice of a passenger seduced by the beauty of the hour was quickly satisfied.

A yawl disembarked us in a narrow cove bordered with chalky cliffs, bright under the pale limpidity of the air. We proposed to reach the summit of the hills, shaped in an amphitheater, which had immediately charmed us.

The heady odor of the Italian coast, a mixture of oranges, myrtles, resin and salt, entered our lungs delightfully. Our little caravan of individuals born in various climes had laid down all burden of personal thought in order to invest itself with the prestige of that lunar excursion, which bore us toward the extreme limits of the domain of sensation, on the edge of the world where human sentiment receives the kiss of the soul of the earth.

We traversed a dense wood of pines in which the breeze sang, and I remember that in the faithful silence, the voice of a sailor shouted: "Hey, where are we, then?"

Then a few paces further away, another profound and young voice said in Italian: "Joy is dead!"

The shiver of that remark broke the harmony that linked me to my companions, and, under the weight of confused impressions, I slowed my pace, with the result that half an hour later, I found myself alone in a star of the wood. I lay down on the ground. The night was mourning the lost suns in the branches. Did I go to sleep or did I stay awake? I no longer know. My body remained beneath the pines but I departed elsewhere—to what point in space, in what era of time?

Many a time, since that night of dream, it has imposed itself on my memory, that indelible vision of my mind's eyes, stronger and more sensitive than those of my flesh. In a lamentable shelter, a wooden carcass clad in ragged sackcloth, a kind of leprous Moor was nestled, enveloped in blue cloth. In front of him, on a table of planks, a metal tray displayed a few coins extracted from the pity of passers-by.

Was it a man, that formless monster, that hideous work of an unhinged demiurge? Through the holes in his rags sprang fuliginous lumps, once flesh. The shiny, swollen stumps, like crabs' pincers, that had once been hands, were crossed over a chaplet. Human hands, the sublime instrument of all labor, of creation and caresses, florid with gestures, the heroic palms of the strong, the pale fingers of lovers, so dear to kiss, those things once resembled you! And that was a face, that chaos of bony caverns and brown blisters, that mask of an empusa framed by rags! Yes, for even that horror radiated a memory of beauty.

"*Ave Maria!*" clamored the harsh voice of the Moor. "*Ave Maria!*"

And his eyes gazed at me, as beautiful as light. Like the spirits of the sun contained in coal, a power of glory was revealed by those great dark eyes, intact and flamboyant, strong with a strange juvenility. I had penetrated into that gaze as into an abyss of anguish, and its vertigo still reached me. It bore me away to the mystery of human suffering, to the world of tears and despairs, to the heart of Erebus. It initiated me into the arcana of a supreme emotion. After that gaze, I had known the secrets of Hell, and I cannot forget them. Yes, all the serenity of my thought remains wounded by them. Like a bullet lodged in generous flesh, the gaze of the demonic Moor is stuck in my soul, in my soul. cleansed nevertheless of doubt, and so proud of its renascence in the certain life...

Will other eyes look at me one day: divinely pure eyes?

THE REDEMPTRIX

To Madame H. Agopian-Pacha[13]

> And there appeared a great wonder
> in Heaven, a woman clothed with
> the sun, and the moon under her
> feet, and upon her head a crown
> of twelve stars.
> (*Revelation* XII: 1)

Oh, gilded flower of my ideal, you bloom too high for my hand ever to pluck you.

Certainly, my gaze has never quit you, but it is with an irremediable despair that that from below—from below forever!—I see your silhouette flamboyant on the horizon of my dream.

And I go forth, I go through life, groping for obstacles, rubbing shoulders with men whose natal baseness I disdain. I march in darkness, the density of which oppresses me and stifles me. And I sense that the darkness will not be illuminated again, whatever happens, that I shall turn around in the obscurity of a funerary crypt.

---

[13] *Tout-Paris*, the directory of Parisian society, lists a Madame Agopian-Pacha as a resident of 95 Boulevard Malesherbes around the end of the nineteenth century. She is mentioned elsewhere as a purchaser of a painting exhibited at the Paros Salon in 1897.

Certain kabbalists claim that many men are dead, who believe that they are alive because they have conserved the appearances of life. Perhaps I am one of those men. My soul has departed with *her*, when she disappeared. Oh, I felt the wing of distress pass over my forehead on that day, the day on which I saw her for the last time. Since then, I have been a dead man walking.

How can I talk about *her?* How can I express in words the impression that her presence gave me? It was the fête of my life. Her aspect multiplied my energies. Existing in her atmosphere, I was conscious of inhabiting a world in which the soul blossomed in bliss. Her person suggested joy, certainty and strength. On seeing her, I understood what theologians call the real presence.

I have lived. Now I am almost old. For having known that creature, what thanks do I not owe to destiny? Often, before the happiness of seeing her had illuminated my sad heart, I envied men whose powers permitted them to march in the orbit of a sublime being. To live in the radiation of a hero; to be a disciple blindly trusting a tranquil and strong master; to be a frail John whose head leaned on the serene shoulder of a Jesus—how many times did I sigh after that possibility?

I have envied you, poor fishermen to whom the mere gesture of the Nazarene Master opened the golden door of total Knowledge.

For I am not a demigod. Although my ideal is higher than that of other men, I remain at their level. I was a seagull whose wings devoid of feathers extended toward the immensity, without the power to soar there.

Now, *she* appeared. I approached her. And all the embryonic forces within me stirred. My most obscure virtualities were manifest in deeds. I cannot imagine an intensity equal to the one I felt in her radiation. Yes, I tell you, my sensibility had joy, my intelligence certainty, my will power. Who was she? An incarnation, a human appearance radiating Wellbeing.

In truth, to remember the man that I was before her coming it requires a painful effort. For I date from the friction of her dress on my life. I had suffered a great deal, I had studied a great deal. I knew all the science of scholars—which is to say, nothing.

I ought to note how my thought was occupied with her for the first time. In what fashion did I succeed in making myself understood? For me, whom she deigned to initiate with a gaze to the most inviolable arcana of life and death, for me, before whom her forbearance opened the five doors of light by means of which one enters the world of causes, for me, all the events contingent to her mysterious existence appeared in the lucidity of absolute logic. But would people understand them? I feel in regard to them like an older brother who is making a little child a portrait of the adorable deceased other whom his adolescence knew. No matter! I shall say how, for the first time, my thought was occupied with *her*.

There was an annunciation of her advent. One night, I had stayed up late poring over an old folio volume of anxious science. Two o'clock had just chimed on the clock of Notre-Dame-des-Champs, of which my house was a neighbor. The weather was stormy, heavy and oppressive. I had shut the window. Heavy Oriental drapes hung along the four walls of my room, in order to isolate my frequent meditations from the exterior world. At that moment I had pushed away my book in order to write notes. I heard a slight continuous rustle.

It's a moth, I said to myself, *which came in while the window was open.*

I lifted up my lamp in order to illuminate the whole room. Not having perceived anything, I resumed writing.

When I raised my head again, stupor held me motionless in my armchair. In front of me, in the lamplight, an extraordinary vision had invaded my room: a naked woman standing on a sphinx. I perceived all the details of that phantasm with an extraordinary precision. The sphinx appeared to be a living animal, of a volume almost equal to that of a horse. Oh, it really was the sibylline beast whose claw oppressed the courageous breast of Oedipus.

It was moving slowly through the air, its vast wings deployed with grace and strength. Its body, as white as marble, was quivering with tamed energy. My imagination, accustomed to represent that allegorical monster in the serene immobility that the sculptors of ancient Egypt attributed to it, was astonished at first to see the vibration of an intense supernatural life in that being, in that human head, of a dolorous and tranquil beauty, in its taurean flanks, in its lion's paws, an in its eagle's wings, which were bumping into the walls of my room as if impatient for limitless space.

On that mount, the young woman was standing calmly. Oh, the strange beauty! The slenderness of her body, the marvelous oval of her face, and, amid the dark undulations of her hair, the gilded pallor of her complexion! An expression of superhuman energy spread in a divine softness, an audacity of innocent domination radiated from that head, from the black profundities of the eyes, from the sinuosity of the lips and the heroic outline of the chin.

The Visitor was brushing the back of the sphinx with her placid feet as a goddess might caress the pale sphere of a world with an indulgent toe. A sidereal rider, she had tamed in the blink of an eye the pride of the hi-erogrammatic animal, which, abjuring any attempt at prancing and any whim of revolt, was prepared to carry the mystery of that victorious will into the infinite with a thrust of its submissive wings.

That conquering beauty invaded my entire soul with an irresistible and suave vehemence. She did not seem to me to be a woman. Her magnificent nudity did not awaken any amour or desire in me. Oh, I remember that, in that minute, an intimate revolution changed the face of my being. Immediately, I felt the analytical faculties from which I had drawn vanity abolished. My intelligence awoke in a renascence. My soul was washed by a lustral water, which impregnated it with enthusiasm, power and plenitude. Life enveloped it like a diaphanous mantle.

Certainly, that apparition, which was to have a definitive influence over my destiny, constituted what the vulgar call a hallucination. But what is a hallucination, if not the projection, on the visible plane, of an invisible reality obedient to the call of our imagination? My thought creates that which it affirms; and are the Platonists not right to consider ideas and images as alive, immortal daughters of the spirit, emanations of the eternal Word? In any case, the distinction that one is accustomed to make between reality and unreality seems to me to be an insult to the subtlety of intelligence so coarse that I shall not deign to linger upon it. Is not reality a subjective creation of the mind that perceives it? Oh, whatever you were, exalting vision, your mere proximity had overturned my soul.

O dominatrix,

You have entered, triumphant and mild, into my ecstatic soul like a beloved king into a village in fête. As soon as the revelation of your possibility, as soon as the caress of your image, as soon as your annunciation, I have cried toward you from the depths of my distress. A gesture of your right hand has opened my eyes. Into the field of my mind you threw the seed of a world. You were Royalty, Glory and Strength.

O liberatrix,

You have entered, triumphant and mild, into my ecstatic soul like a savior warrior into an enslaved town. In the darkness in which my servitude was languishing you brought torches and starlight. The demon of doubt that was gnawing my breast, you expelled with a sign, and your venerated hand has broken my shackles. You summoned Light to my forehead. You were the Truth, the Way and the Life

O consolatrix,

You have entered, triumphant and mild, into my ecstatic soul like a blessed hero into a city in dread. The intoxication of marching in the wake of your robe has charmed all my woes. Your gaze has melted the burden of the dolorous past, which weighed upon my shoulder. Your smile is the flower that confirms life. You were Joy, Hope and Amour.

From the day when that vision came to me, I no longer had any but one desire: to see that creature, whose existence in this world I sensed; to see her and attach myself to her footsteps. The goal of life was flamboyant before my eyes. The goal of life was to march in the circle of her gaze, was to be impregnated by her radiation, was to respire her emanation.

The irresistible impulsion that projected me toward that woman was not sexual amour. In the impetuosity of my youth, amour had watered me with all its delights and all its anguish; but this Unknown Woman had invaded me with a sentiment analogous to the one that believers have for their god, that of Magdalen for Jesus, that of Saint Theresa for the Crucified. For me she was the Divine made flesh. She was an abyss of light into which I rolled recklessly.

Where would I see her? For surely she existed. In what place in the world would it be given to me to approach her sublime silhouette? Sometimes, a horrible anguish gripped me. What if I were never to see her? What if she had manifested herself thus to me uniquely? To glimpse that mysterious mirage for an instant, to understand in certainty that she existed, and never to contemplate her sacred feet! Perhaps I was not worthy of her presence? I passed through all the graduated alternatives of hope and despair.

At all hazard, and even though an intimate voice cried to me that such a creature laughed at distance, that she was not enslaved, like the rest of us, by the norms of space, I was always ready to depart; I was always ready to run, at the top speed of present means of locomotion, toward the country that possessed her aspect.

One morning, I received an invitation to an intimate tea at the home of Madame X***. The name was unknown to me. I threw the letter on the table indifferently, with the intention of sending the woman my card. I had completely forgotten that incident of a mundane order when the appointed evening arrived. An irresistible need then invaded me to render to that invitation. I dressed in haste, and an hour later I arrived in the small town house in which Madame X*** lived, very close to the foliage of the Bois de Boulogne.

As soon as I crossed the threshold of the drawing room, an emotion took possession of me. *She* was there. Yes, this time it was really her, alive and similar to the apparition that had bowled me over. As on the night of the annunciation, I sensed a superhuman expansion within me, a heroic exaltation of my entire being. In less than a second, I perceived everything that was happening in the drawing room, and I penetrated its mystery. Why is it necessary for me, in order to try to give an impression of it today, only to be able to use the cold and impotent succession of words?

Isiah, your breath has vivified my breast. In order to speak about you, to evoke your essence, give your faithful follower the force of genius and the speech of the Prophets! In order to confide to the world a pale exoteric notion of what their gentle Master was, the four evangelists, the quaternary of disciples who accompanied the Lion, the Angel, the Eagle and the Bull have clad the esoteric allegory of their story in simplicity. Alone on Patmos, John revealed, under the veil of a higher symbolism, the fulgurant Word that only Initiates understand. Isiah, in order for your reign to arrive, others will announce your Word in the due form. I shall simply say what you enabled in me.

Isiah spoke, standing up, in a circle of listeners avid for her voice.

She was dressed in a white robe of Chinese crepe, the admirable organization of which and the profound esthematic[14] would have discouraged the most expert Parisian couturiers. Over the right skirt, pressed by a very light gathering, ran the pleats of a bodice garnished with silver embroideries, the modern arrangement of which evoked a memory of the peplum. Delicately opened over the masculine beauty of the throat, the undulating pleats of that bodice permitted the body of the woman a sumptuous liberty of attitudes, seemingly maintained by a silver cord around the waist, the curve of which they accompanied in order to fade away along the skirt.

With the sudden lucidity that the proximity of that creature inspired in me, I understood the symbolism of that evening dress, marrying the vestimental forms of the Orient and the Occident, and charged with silver, the lunar and feminine metal.

A glance over the members of the audience alerted me to all their idiosyncrasy. There were some twenty men and women there, belonging to different social categories. Amid the luxury of that drawing room there were men of the people, and also those people that society calls *déclassé*, with foreheads too high to pass under the low doors that led to the cowsheds of the flourishing mediocrity, breasts inflated by an idea that only emerges in sobs! All had faces sealed by suffering; and I sensed that those men were my brothers.

Desolate hearts: some, on the threshold of a chagrined maturity had been tossed harshly by the swell of

---

[14] The slightly esoteric term *esthematique* [esthematic] is defined in Nicolas Bescherelle's 1845 dictionary as "pertaining to costume." It was briefly popularized by Octave Uzanne in the title of a history of French fashion, but Michelet's story predates that 1897 text.

life; others, on the threshold of their adolescence, had resorbed their efflorescence, alarmed with a sacred fear by an intuition of the dolors of life. Oh, like mine; those hearts had groaned toward the serenity of a faith; they had all palpitated toward a master who would orientate definitively the nobility of their essential impetus, who would guide toward an unknown sky the quivering wings of their will.

There were sad young women. There was a weary courtesan whose soul no one had fathomed, and who ennobled the charity of having offered to the unfortunate the consoling flower of her beauty. There was a noble virgin, lamentable in not having encountered on earth the elect of her dream; and also a woman bewildered by bearing in her loins the immortal wound of her betrayed amour. There was a mother from whom the tomb had stolen seven children. And among them was the mistress of the house, Madame X***. She was a woman of about thirty, of an unhealthy elegance. I read in her faded blue eyes the dolorous secret of her past, and I bent over to kiss her meager hand.

A glory of morning magnified the foreheads of the men, whom destiny had treated differently. Some were simple, accustomed to daily labor. There was a pastor with eyes enlarged by the kiss of the stars; a pale miner whose deformed body developed the awkward gesture of nocturnal beasts; a sailor whose rude mask was resplendent with the nobility that the habit of braving danger imprints. Children of the sea, the earth and the sky; weary bodies, candid hearts, and new heads; no social hypocrisy, no conventional baseness, and no fallacious education had assaulted the august liberty of their instinct. Having known no other masters than nature and tribulation, their intact souls were ready to understand everything.

There was an orator, a generous homilist of revolt, who, shaking off the resignation of the poor and the oppressed, had clamored toward a vision of justice, had extended the anger of his vibrant fists toward the ignominy of the rich and powerful. There was a very young dreamer whose admirable solar beauty was radiant with genius. Others, in sum, whom life had disappointed: a flock of bleeding souls in quest of a pastor with saving hands.

We were twenty and one around Isiah, all still young.

Oh, that evening of my life embalmed me for eternity; I had the sentiment of being, in a glorious flesh, a divine soul. And likewise were the twenty companions of my ecstasy. A total revivification had effaced the anguishes of nature, as if Isiah's magnificent hand had extended toward their ardent nostrils the azure flower of nepenthe, from which one inhales forgetfulness. All lovers of an illuminative existence, we were liberated from Time, Number and Space and we were floating in the Eternal with the vertigo of eaglets trying their wings in the liberty of the skies.

And I heard *her* voice, her silence already expanded over me, with a torrential force, her infinite thought. But the music of that thought, that adorable speech, awoke in me the plenitude of a somnolent world. And I saw *her* body, a radiant symbol of her soul. She had given the scepter of her hand to our lips, a hand sculpted for power and superhuman audacity. Then I understood the charm with which she enveloped beings. In her, there was nothing that was not in accordance with the perfect Rhythm, rhythm being the most direct expression of the

Word. She was all harmony, and her grace realized the immutable logic of her potentialities.

There was an organ in the room. Isiah sat down at the keyboard, and I had the revelation of Music, that angelic language capable of concentrating in a definitive formula the most mysterious vibrations of human being and worlds. For music is to speech what Amour is to Thought, what the eagle is to the cricket. Beyond speech, a narrow hood shaped to fit a single idea corseted with precision, it is a cloak vast enough to shelter the unlimited aspiration of being; it is the monstrous voice that sings the exegesis of the infinite.

But all the music I had known, what was it? An infantile stammer! The vehement fervor of Bach, the somber anxiety of Beethoven, the passion of Wagner and all those beautiful cries of genius in the parturition of a dream, how frail and frozen they appeared to me!

In that ineffable evening, my soul, in flight in the mysterious orbit of sonorities, perceived the total Revelation. Yes. I lived harmony. Rhythm carried me away, a bewildered corybant, into the sphere of the angels, and, my eyes dazzled by wild light, I rolled in the golden egg where the gods involve.

Scarcely had Isiah run her fingers over the keys than we all felt a solemn and vertiginous frisson run through us. That new music bathed us, washed away our past, enveloped us with rebirth. In order to uncover for us there and then the limitless horizon of her soul, Isiah spoke to us in the seraphic language in which the mystery of her essence became a parable. On the cheeks of my companions, pale with a sacred pallor, slow tears trickled, the dew of a spiritual dawn.

Who, then, would have the derisory pretention of analyzing that hymn? To begin with it sang, formidably, all our past sufferings, intimately precise and all fused together in the immensity of human dolor. But while showing us the withering memory, it transported us to a mountain of bliss, like prisoners contemplating from the height of a sunlit summit the somber city in which yesterday's prison stood. Then, launched from that black world to rise toward a world of whiteness, we had the sensation of soaring, spirits under full sail, through cycles of eternal wellbeing, which she filled with her triumphant presence.

The finale was vibrating within us when Isiah stood up. Every amorous emotion is made of a delight and an anguish. In our rapturous minds an anguish became sharp: was *she* about to quit us? After being manifest, a sun in the darkness, might she not vanish, leaving in our charmed eyes the regret of the adored vision? For none of us could any longer conceive life without *her*.

She calmed our dread with a smile, and spoke.

"Friends, we are going to live together, in a solitary land where no noise of the world will trouble our peace. You will be alerted when the time has come. Let serenity be within you, and strength, for you are the elect of a mysterious destiny.

A gesture of her bright hands and I no longer saw *her*. In the room, we remained mute, but the benediction of the creature lived within us, delectably.

A supper awaited us. No one dared raise his voice for fear of alarming the silence, full of dreams of having known her. I tried to interrogate Madame X***. She looked at me with consoled eyes, without responding.

The railway deposited us, on a light evening in spring, on the edge of a high forest extended over the side of a hill. We found one another again, the twenty and one companions of the memorable evening, in the delight of our common secret, and we exchanged the kiss of our gazes. We knew that it was necessary to traverse the forest. We walked along a winding path at a brisk pace without pronouncing a word. All vibrant with the same sentiment, it was not necessary to awaken the debilitated echo of it. And we had the intuition of being a single collective soul living the same thought, absorbing the same amour.

The shadow enveloped us. The woodland voices of which, in the course of my childhood walks, I had heard the sinister buzz, shivering—the intermittent voices in which are scattered the rustling of leaves, the creaking of stems and the noises of nocturnal insects—accompanied the beating of our hearts. And we raised our heads in the expectation of seeing, between the black masses of foliage, the flamboyant star descend that would guide our march toward *her*.

We reached the summit of the hill, from which we could hear the sea growling. There was a house among the trees. That was it. A door opened of its own accord, and we penetrated into the hoped-for refuge, shaking off with the dust of our soles all the anguish of the evanescent past.

Poverty, the poverty of human aspiration! When Psyche possessed Eros in nocturnal mystery, she had happiness. What did derisory curiosity matter? No, it was necessary that she abandon her heart in fête to the insidious demon of anxiety. And am I not, by virtue of natal impulsion, a simple soul? Why did the stars that scintillated over my cradle deprive me of heroic and credulous candor?

Isiah, when my bosom was resplendent under your gaze like a helm of steel under the fires of the sun, I occupied the supreme peace, the peace promised to men of god will. But your absence was the return of darkness. In the hours when I no longer sensed upon me the influx of your will, I yielded to the phantom of curious distress. I desired to know the key to the divine enigma that was You. I allowed the armor of my faith to be corroded. And that is why I lost the gleam of your trace.

It was during the morning meal on the day after our arrival in that blessed house. We were gathered around a vast table. In the frame of the windows, we perceived the sunlit sea. It seemed to us that we would have been able, behind *her*, to walk on those waves all the way to the horizon, beyond which the fatherland of our hopes might be resplendent.

She was wearing a pale blue robe, in linen cloth, the loose pleats of which broadcast quietude to us. Blue, the color of Amour, inspires calm in sick souls. A golden belt rose toward her breasts. She exercised her hospitality with a sovereign grace. Croaz, the sailor, was sitting to her right, Heliel, the handsome young poet, whose gilded eyes reflected the bewildered dream of being enchained to her gesture, to her left.

A glad silence floated over us. Who would have dared to break with a voice the charm scattered in our confidence? And we ate the bread as if her lips had said: "Eat, this is my flesh."

An impenetrable meditation darkened Isiah's beautiful forehead, but without tarnishing the golden radiation that our sharpened senses perceived around her dark tresses. A tear was suspended on the velvet of her eyelashes, and there was the heavy flight of a distress over us. Suffering, then, could bite into the marble of that bosom, in which our strength resided.

She had a divinely sad smile.

"Friends," she said, "children of my election, I am suffering your suffering. Forgive my forehead for being morose. I have woven a crown for it of all the thorns that will wound you. I am weeping for your future dolor in losing me. For you will lose my appearance. Alas, your curiosity will chase me away from you. Thus the Law wishes it.

We shivered. Heliel let his desperate hands fall upon the table. "Oh!" he said. "I believed in the eternity of seeing you!"

He expressed our sentiment; for our hearts were vibrating in unison, and each of us was a string of a unique lyre, of which the finger of Isiah revealed the harmonious soul.

"Heliel! What cloud is enveloping your genius? Have you forgotten, then, why you are here? Poet, gentle missionary of the Word, be able to support the bitterness of exile in a world where you are not heard. Your voice reveals beauty and amour, two of the highest manifestations of the gods. And since it announces the word of the gods, who will understand it among humans that have renounced the energy of belief? No matter; you will do your duty of a Hero. You will sing, like your brother Orpheus, among the beasts; you will reflect light, son of the Sun, upon the somber children of Saturn."

"Isiah! No, I can no longer forget the Causes. I was summoned to your presence in order that an inextinguishable enthusiasm should set my life as an apostle ablaze."

"None of your gestures is devoid of a cause, as none is devoid of an effect. If each of you was chosen to come to me, it is by virtue of immemorial reasons of which I know the origins. In all of you, dolor exalted life. Each of you is a link in a chain that still attaches me to the earth. I was sent here for a mission. I shall direct the course of the river of your allied wills toward the ocean of mystery."

"Isiah," I asked, trembling like a child, "Jesus of Nazareth was the son of God. Alas, we are no longer able to adore the bloody feet of Jesus. Are you, Isiah, the daughter of God?"

"Jesus, my supreme brother, has said: 'I inform you making use of the speech of the earth, and you do not hear me; how would you be able to understand me if I spoke the language of Heaven?' And I say to you: every man is the son of God; all living flesh is the symbol of a divine thought. Every man is an Adam summoned to become a Christos. He is three Adams. Meditate, and you will understand the meaning of words. Now, beings are born who have a more profound revelation of the Truth. They arrive on earth, from time to time, delegated and sanctified, in order to show humans the increate Light. They do not fasten all the sails with which destiny covers them, for mortal eyes would be burned by their glare. When Moses descended from Sinai, having contemplated the increate Light, he knew that humans would be unable to support the dazzling reflection on his brow, and he hid his face with a flap of his cloak. The Revelators, his sacred brethren, the Buddha, Mahomet, the Báb and all the Messiahs lifted over the world, in their predestined fists, the torch that each of them had lit from the same resplendent hearth. But if they had unveiled the naked glory of the hearth itself, they would have blinded the eyes of races. To the unique and eternal Truth they built sanctuaries of different architectures.

They sang the same hymn in various languages. And when they expired, voluntary victims, their last breath swept away one of the clouds interposed between the planet and the absolute. The supreme breath of the Crucified tears the veil that covers the Temple. He has given a part of the world the keys of the initiation."

Her voice carried us away like a river of force. Having reposed the gleam of her yes in a vision, she went on: "I have come to you in order to put you on the path. Then I shall return."

Her head tilted toward her shoulder. Her beauty seemed to us more profound than the Heavens. Our hands came together, extended toward her. Sobs rose up from our group,

"Isiah! Isiah! Don't leave us!"

Her voice caressed us: "Friends, it will be my good fortune to suffer for you. The Law is ineluctable: the initiator perishes by the initiate."

Her smile melted our anguish. An enthusiasm irrupted within us, vaster than the blue sea whose waves we perceived through the window. Oh, to live, to live that hour...

The worlds were as transparent for us as globes of crystal, and we existed in the power.

Heliel's voice formulated our thought, our gratitude and our hope:

"O Revelatrix,

"I salute you outside Time, for I know you in the Eternal. You exist, O daughter of God. O supreme symbol of femininity. The Ancient of Days is your father and you were engendered in the womb of the Divine Mother. You are the silver cup in which my charmed soul drinks—Salut!

"O Salvatrix,

"I salute you, you come to us with hands full of graces and fingers extended for benedictions, bearing the ring of amour and the ring of forgetfulness that Moses forged. Between your breasts, suspended from your silver necklace, the seven talismans repose that caressed the vapor of perfumes flying toward the septenary of planets. And your eyes are gentler to wounds than oil and wine.

"O Redemptrix,

"I salute you. In tearing from our gaze the veil that hid the light, you charged your beautiful forehead with our heavy sins. All the weaknesses of our frail wills, you assume, adorable starveling of sacrifice; and the palest of our smiles to Sathan is an arrow that goes to pierce your bosom. Triumphatrix of suffering, I salute you in the glorious eternity in which you are enthroned, near Horus, to the left of Isis.

"Your Name is a Mystery. Your Age is a Mystery. You count thirty-three years; for you have meditated during the twelve hours and you have accomplished the twelve labors. Into the calm palace of your breast, the five infernal torments have rushed: Bitterness, Pain, Darkness, inextinguishable Ardor and penetrating Putrescence. And, smiling, you trample under your victorious foot the four demons of the elements who howl at the four corners of the world: Samael, prince of Salamanders; Azazel, prince of Sylphs; Azael, prince of Undines; and Mahazahel, prince of Gnomes.

"You are a Mystery yourself. You emerge from the heart of God in order to bring us back to him. Sons of the Fall, children in exile, we will rise again in your wake toward the bosom of our father. Eyes of the light of your glory, we shall evolve, through supracelestial

133

cycles, having scorned the ambushes of serpents, dogs and fire. You will give us the strength to defeat the Dragon Nahasch, which guards the gates of Heaven, and we shall pass, clad in joy, through the sonorous flights of the Angels, the Cherubim and the Seraphim, toward the throne of musical gems where you reign, contemplating the repose of the cohorts of Fire.

The hours passed, as caressant as mothers. The hours! What scorn we had for that habitual human conception! Time, that lamentable division of eternity! We were delivered from its embrace. Our spirits moved in a limitless liberty, and our eyes were able to see effects in causes.

Her presence enveloped us in wellbeing. How sweet the air was in our lungs during walks along the sea shore, when her voice enchanted our souls; I would toil in vain in the attempt to evoke our bliss. Happiness is indescribable. I, who have known it, who have lived it, would not be able to awaken the palest reflection of it in the mirror of words that I present to humans. The most luminous poets and the most vertiginous musicians have blunted their genius on that impossibility. No matter how magnificently they translate the cry of dolor, none of them has been able to hurl in the face of the sun the triumphal hymn of happiness. The chain is mysterious that retains their flight in the song of felicity. If the most sublime of those heroes succeeded in incarnating in the living body of a poem the idea of the wellbeing contained in the heart of the infinite, if the Prometheus in question stole that flame from the bosom of the gods, the intoxicated earth would possess, enchained in form, the very soul of that wellbeing, and humankind would desert the path of suffering into which it has been forced by destiny.

One day, we were walking at the fall of dusk. A fresh sea breeze was blowing and the moon, still pale, surged forth in a mist that was softening the contours of things. I was giving my arm to one of our companions, an admirable redhead whose youth had mourned futile beauty. We were all waking in groups behind Isiah, whose meditation we were respecting. Our eyes never quit the silhouette, the juvenile magnificence of which was enveloped by a vague mantle of Aeolian lilac; and in the ash-blue evening, the pale scintillation of flecks of gold dotted in the mantle of lace caressing her dark hair, appeared to me to be the glimmer of a holy star over the sinister path.

We arrived in a ravine planted with bushes and brambles. Isiah was sitting on a corner of rock. We lay down around her feet. A disturbance was haunting me, but I dared not speak. She enveloped me with her tender gaze.

"You will be cured of your malady one day; you are suffering for having respired the surrounding air since birth."

"Your hand on my forehead, Isiah, has expelled all my illness"

"Learn Faith! Learn Amour! Learn to magnify yourself. Alas, you count on me too much, my friends, and your feeble hearts are suspended on my lips. You hope that my finger, striking the rock, will make the spring gush forth in which you can drink the living water, and you do not extend your strength toward the required effort. But my wings cannot carry you asleep into the heaven of your aspirations. No one is redeemed other than by himself. No one will attain the summit of universal life without having bloodied his feet on the stones of the road. I am showing you the way. March! Create your paradisal atmosphere, my friends."

Our eyes begged her. She gazed at the nocturnal vault in which the stars were lighting up.

"I exist to bring strength to your bosoms. You have suffered for having lived in a time of cowardice. For unbelief and absence of amour are daughters of cowardice. All skepticism is a weakness, as vile as fear. All Faith and all Amour are the courage of the will in parturition of its divine becoming. Osiris is a black god, but you will be gods if you wish."

She had risen to her feet. Now she stood out, a mysterious silhouette, against the velvet of the night. Her voice had the suave force of the music that she had revealed.

"Have Amour, and you will understand Number. On the day fixed by destiny, when a new Sign reigns over the earth, when the Four will be succeeded by the Five, when the Flamboyant star will rise over the sphere instead of the Cross, humans will disdain the vanity of thought for the evident Amour. They will possess the Amour that gives Sight, and they will see and hear, and currents that will girdle the planet that will ferry Amour. Friends, you to whom I have revealed the superhuman path, hurl yourselves into amour, recklessly. Amour, creator of worlds, is manifest in two powers, Belief and Prayer, the two supreme energies of will. The man in whom the Prayer lives will march, clad in joy over the seven Spheres, and *his flesh will become Word*. Prayer is the action of Will upon the world. It directs forces, commands the elements; it manipulates the lightning known to Seers alone. But those alone possess Prayer in the sanctuary of their breasts who accomplish the quadruple duty announced by the Sphinx: know, dare, will, fall silent. Those, Prayer guides, with its fulgurant glare, into the somber temple of mystery. O brethren of my election, love, believe and pray. You are twenty and one and we are twenty-two. There are twenty-two arcana. Unite in Amour and you will be the chain that will attach to the world the Sign that I bring in my vaulted hands. For humankind is led toward its ends by the virtue of Signs that it does not know."

During a pause, the face of the revelatrix subsided into a heroic anguish. A mysterious combat was taking place in the depths of her silence. A sharp intuition traversed my heart like a sword-thrust. It seemed to us that the evening breeze was bringing us, from the heart of the Invisible where all that exists is conserved, the total comprehension of the unspeakable dolor of which the solitary Garden of Olives was witness beneath the veil of a pale evening. Oh, all the majesty of an angelic suffering enveloped the beauty of that creature. In the glimmer of starlight, the infinitely subtle nuances of her flesh were effaced. Our gazes only perceived the black velvet of the eyes amid the darkened whiteness of the profile, whose pure design, superb in the slightly aquiline nose, audacious in the mouth, sovereignly strong in the chin, was outlined in a gilded glory bathing the hair. That was the duration of an eagle taking flight. The triumph of the will dressed that noble head with splendor, and those hands, those ghostly hands...

"The hour has come when you will not see me any longer. Friends, hold out your foreheads, that my hands might summon the caress of life, the clemency of death and the emprise of eternity thereto. Adieu, beloved hearts, human hearts that dolor has washed with its corrosive waves. Why is it not given to me to efface past

137

wounds forever? Let my blood be the lustral water, the living water from which you emerge penetrated by invincible hope! Adieu, renewed hearts! I bless in you rosy Orients from which the sun of universal amour will surge.

"You are the beautiful thoughts of the earth, the earth that is a beautiful thought of the Eternal. Adieu, earth from which I am passing. May my trace remain in your flank, as luminous as a lighthouse indicating the port to its bruised children! Adieu, earth to which I came in order to suffer. May you erect on your horizon the vivifying Sign that I have the mission of revealing to you, washed with my blood as it was torn from my heart!

"Adieu, Earth; you seem a soiled fatherland; on your face, the genius is mocked, the just man torn apart, the weak crushed, beauty insulted, the gods blasphemed. The echo of your mountains sends back to the holy stars the clamor of the stifled poet, the flagellated saint, the violated virgin and the poor starveling. You are, however, a chaste fatherland. You nourish souls of devotion. I salute you in your prophets, your victims and your martyrs. You are a noble fatherland, for, to those born on your soil, you can give the crowns of genius, beauty, sacrifice and dolor. The heroism of a few of your sons intercedes for you in the visible; and I, with my mysterious brethren, who die on the cross, summon with my wounded hands the infinity of the increate Light upon our expanded bosom. Adieu, flower of the infinite of which I am bringing the perfume to the feet of God."

The day after that evening we did not attempt to look for her. We knew that her appearance was abolished. We exchanged gazes of a serene sadness. Oh, it was doubtless for us that her adorable flesh was suffering in some desert. Alas, with what ardor we would have offered our common soul to infernal torments, the very soul of our twenty and one forms, in order to save a hair of her sweet head! We did not see her again, but her presence lived in us like a star of force.

We wandered, souls in joy and in pain, over the sand of the shore.

It was the third morning.

We saw—yes, we saw, with our eyes from which the scales had fallen, the eyes of Seers. The sun was rising over the sea, a vaporous and gilded sun. The plain of the tranquil waves was spread out, an immensity of pale gold that volatilized at the horizon toward the light vault of the sky. On the rutilant and distant disk of the star, oh, vision of terror...her beautiful head was tilted over her shoulder, blanched by dolor; her hair was a mantle of mourning flowing toward her bloodless feet. And her body, that admirable body, was nailed on a cross, wounded, broken, stained with pale blood, weakening under the blows of torture and death.

Slowly, the crucial apparition sank into the waves.

Now, in the solemn ascension of the zenith, the entire circle of the sun emerged, flamboyant with red gold.

And there was a second vision.

Inscribed on the disk touching the marine horizon, a majestic silver star with five points appeared, like a section of a blazon of mystery. The star had a point at the top, two at the bottom, one to the right and one to the left. And upon that Sign *she* sprang forth, vertical, extending her marvelous horizontally toward the two points of the star. And the sun made an aureole for her glorious flesh, for her sacred nudity. Her head—oh, so luminously beautiful in her nocturnal hair—was held high, radiating triumph, ablaze with her gaze, directed toward the heavens, all of whose arcana she possessed, toward the infinity of worlds, her eternal fatherland.

Star of divine wellbeing...

And since then, I live, I march, passing nostalgically over this planet; and I am still waiting, waiting...

AMOROUS MAGIC

To Octave Mirbeau

To live in the uniquely real world of the Idea.
Richard Wagner.

Leaning on the balustrade of the terrace, they were both listening to the languid noise of the waves rising in the charm of the summer night.

Inattentive to the counsel of bliss emanating from the nocturnal mildness, however, the young man was staring intently, by the pale light of the violet stars, at the brow of his beloved companion.

He wanted to break the pensive mutism of their mouths.

"Dear flower of amour, you're not unaware that I always hear your silence; at this hour, my mind is following anxiously, in all its evolutions, the worry that is spreading its shadow in your heart, and yet I'm suffering because you have not made me the confession of it."

Eager to spare that faithful solicitude the chagrin that she sensed born therein, she turned her face toward her friend, illuminated by a tranquil smile.

"Friend, your tenderness becomes anxious too easily. No worry haunts me, and I love you."

He put his arms around her, still melancholy, and then slowly approached the young woman's long eyelashes, under the constant ardor of his lips.

"Gerberte, your generous tenderness is striving to inspire in me the illusion of a serenity that is not within you—but can your sentiments be unknown to me?"

"Yes, forgive me. I know that in the amplitude of your powerful thought my humble womanly impressions vibrate, immensely magnified, like the light fall of a pearl in a cup of fine crystal. Forgive me if, for the first time, I have attempted to hide something of me from you."

"You cannot determine the causes of the trouble, still vague, that is disturbing you. Listen: although our amour is so beautiful that it causes vulgar couples to marvel, it has not been able to give your superior soul all that it demanded of it…oh, don't try to deny it, innocent victim of a mysterious law; the realization, although almost superhuman, remains, by virtue of it monotony, beneath your avid dream. That is why, just now, our eyes were unconsciously interrogating the sea, over which they were wishing for some unknown to arrive, and those stars, which suggest unusual abodes. But I would not think myself worthy of having stirred your dear breast, and I would have renounced, in spite of my immortal dolor, the unique happiness of possessing your dear life, if, sincerely sounding my forces, I did not think myself capable of satisfying the most distant of your desires as soon as it awakes. The shadow of sadness that I have seen passing over the limpidity of your face for the first time since our amour, I shall drive away. You shall walk your fulfilled dreams, triumphantly like beautiful submissive greyhounds, through seemingly impossible Edens. Come, look me in the eyes for a long time…"

Proudly obedient, the young woman rested her frail hand on the beloved's shoulder, as if for a waltz, and then offered her bright agate irises, in which a confident smile was fading, to the bright eyes that were appealing to her.

They remained thus for a few moments. Gerberte's eyelids fluttered, like the wings of wounded birds, and finally remained lowered, while she murmured, in a voice whose ordinary music was strangely muffled: "Pierre...that's singular...what do you want, then?"

Without responding, he lifted her up in his arms and deposited her, not without a thousand precautions, in the silk hammock extended between two acacias on the terrace.

To that supple couch, on which the starlight indicated the grace of the young body softly, he imprinted a swing as light at the pitching of a junk on a slow river. And there, inaccessible to the voice of the summer night continuing its placid course, and even to the pride of dominating the charming sleeping individual thus, he contemplated the motionless lover, with feverish preoccupations.

"Go!" he said.

And during that time, on the young man's mental order, the sleeping Gerberte's spirit flew toward distant countries in abolished times. It went away, inhabiting legendary shores, incarnate in individuals whose existence was a felicity.

First there were the mysteries of immemorial India; and Gerberte sensed herself living, or having lived, as a glorious queen, in the arms of a sovereign who was her beloved Pierre.

She was seated on a golden throne supported by four bronze dragons with monstrous mouths, ecstatic before the regal beauty of her lover. Around them, jasper columns with silver fluting loomed up on the azure horizon, and before the yellow porphyry steps of the platform on which their toes rested, people were arriving to salute their glory. Subjugated sovereigns brought by the heavy tread of elephants decked with gold prostrated themselves before the motionless feet of the triumphant lovers, and from behind the silently flowing multicolored crowds of vassal nations, respectfully opening a passage for rhapsodies sung to the immortal clemency of the royal couple, groups of admirably beautiful young women spread out in expert dances, their hair scattered, for the joy of the eyes.

Slightly weary of contemplating the spectacle with the rigidity of two metallic gods set in pagodas, the young queen made a sign, and the crowds vanished. She remained alone next to the conqueror of her election, still playfully plunging her golden slipper into the mane of a tame lion.

Opposite the perforated palace, the sun was extinguishing its flames; and after that apparition of multiform life coming to salute them, they both sensed the peace of the evening descending upon their dear isolation: alone with a few scarlet birds that were chattering amid the giant verdure of banana trees; alone with the fresh sound of little waterfalls weeping in basins; and, sometimes, the roar of a marauding tiger.

And Gerberte was exalted in contemplating at her knees that handsome tamer of fatherlands, whose redoubtable scimitar with an adamantine hilt was offered as a plaything to his wife's pale hands. He extended his arms toward her, his eyes full of an ever-

inextinguishable passion. The slight shock of their enlacement caused the streams of emeralds on their breasts
to resonate. Then the unconsciousness of a total bliss
gripped them as soon their lips met...

Meanwhile, on the terrace bordering the sea, dawn
was already paling the stars.

When the young woman woke up in the silk hammock, her astonished eyes perceived, standing beside her
and attentive to her gestures, the man she loved.

After an effort to recover the ordinary clarity of her
thought, she opened her lips for an interrogation.

A caress sealed her mouth.

"Have you known pleasant hours last night,
Gerberte?"

He went on: "That vision, which my imagination
was pleased to offer you, forget it! It isn't worthy to occupy your heart for a minute longer, and I only conceived it in order to distract you momentarily. For you,
noble creature, who, scorning the vanities precious to
inferior humans, believed that only the devotion of an
imperishable amour was worthy of making your blood
beat faster, the dominations and glories that you have
just possessed are, as you know, puerile baubles of
which your frail hands would quickly weary. I only
wanted to amuse you for an hour with the splendor of
something trivial; and you have allowed your elevated
desires to repose on despotic pomp like a hierophant rejoicing momentarily in an exotic trifle. The artificial paradises, less vulgar, in which the flight of your soul
would like to wander, I can conceive, thanks to you, who
have opened the routes to them for me, as Beatrice guided the footsteps of Alighieri mystically."

"Friend, I hear your voice without comprehending it, for I remain dazzled for having lived some implausible tale."

"And if you agree, you will see more than a thousand, for we shall explore the only domain whose limits are distant."

The next day, the young man's will took the sleeping lover to the fortunate isle of Avalon, in times anterior to the ideal reign of King Arthur. There she became intoxicated, before the sacred sea, under the golden efflorescence of unknown trees in an idyll of which nothing injured the constant unity. Pierre's brain had enough poetic strength to invest the young woman's mind with the forgotten candor of young terrestrial centuries.

Supreme joy! She knew a passion inaccessible to any violent impact of beings or things. Gerberte now possessed the plenitude that they had both sought in vain by means of a voluntary exile from contemporary society, against the invasions of which they had raised, as a sold barrier, the august egotism of their mutual love. For the first time, she knew the invulnerable sensual pleasure of a mind that no importunate breath can deflect from its goal; her unique thought, and all of her tenderness, blossomed in fortunate Avalon, a rose that no cold wind could chill.

And it was thus for days.

In the tracks of her powerful guide, Gerberte inhabited imaginary worlds, and was incarnate in characters whose legendary existence she had envied. And Pierre was ingenious in deploying the most perfect conceptions, like a triumphant carpet, for the little feet of the beloved woman. He created poems of magnificent ideality in order to offer his lover the illusion of living them, as other men offer flowers.

Visions of the sumptuous Orient alternated with mystical ecstasies, and Gerberte knew everything for which languishing beings could wish, of noble or curious nostalgias, in these morose times.

Stirred by emotions, she traversed idylls, epics and dramas, among the fantastic sumptuousness of décors. And just as her upper body was enriched with varied ornaments, her soul took on different fashions of thinking and feeling.

Sometimes she was an insouciant daughter of Bohemia, throwing the sonorous bursts of her Basque tambourine and her laughter to the eglantines of the roadside; sometimes she was an amorous illuminate in the snowy lands where swans frolic; sometimes she was an ornamented idol receiving in the depths of a temple, with perfumes burned in cassolettes, the adoration of prostrate crowds.

Thus she intoxicated herself on the mirage of heroic and sentimental life that her early youth had thought naturally possible.

Except that, as a mysterious law chastises whoever denies the customary order of things in order to land in artificial paradises, as every hour of fictitious wellbeing carries within itself the seed of an alternative evil, in her moments of wakefulness, Gerberte stumbled over the reality of which she had lost the sense, like Michelangelo when he descended from the cupola where he was painting his fresco in the Sistine Chapel.

And perhaps, for his part, Pierre became more dolorous in only participating partly in the felicities created for her. Perhaps both of them came to feel, beneath their twin steps, the very ground of their voluntary illusion giving way.

"Dear soul," the young woman said, one day, with her feminine delicacy, "these worlds that your power gives me, it's only your image that inhabits them with me, not your self. That's what I've just realized—and don't you know that no joy can exist for me of which you only have half?"

THE DISQUIETING ROSE

To Madame Berthe Faye

Perhaps every creature, and every object, is merely for us a symbol capable of generating an emotion. We live, among beings and things, armored by custom against their significance, like a man in his natal village who has never traveled. The latter does not possess an exact vision of his locale, since he has never been able to compare it with any other. Thus, it would be necessary to have known other worlds than that of appearances in which we struggle in order to perceive things under their real and unique character of Signs.

Have you observed the disconcerting diversity with which objects play for each of us the role that is assigned to them? Some have awakened emotions in me very different from those that they ordinarily inspire. I remember that the object that revealed to me, not the fear, but the sacred horror, invading our hearts at the moment when the mystery of living appears most oppressive, was a rose—a radiant and delightful rose!

I was then a savage and solitary adolescent who divided his hours between old books and juvenile vagabondage over land and sea in the vicinity of a tiny fishing port in Bretagne. I was wrong to say solitary, for a faithful companion never quit me: my dog Nello, a large black bloodhound with gilded eyes. Few friendships are as perfect as the one uniting Nello and me. Like faith or reason, amour is a mode of accession to knowledge. By the light of loving me, the animal penetrated into the dense virgin forest of my thought, and I loved Nello enough to sense confusedly that his honest bestial ingenuousness was akin to my precocious troubled meditation.

How many times, with him, I paraded my laughing dream between the sea and the stars in an adventurous little boat, the *Minar*! Nello had become a mariner. He was able to haul in a sheet with his mouth and even hold the tiller with his paws.

"Helm to the wind, Nello!" And with a nimble and sure gesture, my quadruped friend did his work as a helmsman, while I followed my train of thought at my ease in the open air.

We had both departed on an excursion on a warm June day. A weak breeze bore the *Minar* gently out to sea. We headed for a sort of islet formed by a single rock some five or six kilometers from the wild coast, which was known as the Heifer because of its vaguely bovine form. I have never known why the local mariners were reluctant to go near that "pebble." It rose up sheerly over a great depth of water, and no breakers bristled in its vicinity.

This time, a whim took me to visit the rock, more accustomed to serve as a station for cormorants than as a pedestal for a human silhouette. I went around it in order to see whether some goat-track formed by the asperities of the granite might permit me to scale its trump, raised about five or six brasses above the high sea, and on which I could perceive a flora of stonecrops and couch-grass. But no cat could ever have climbed those sheer walls.

I had a rope and a crampon. The sea being extremely calm, I was able to moor the boat to the stone without risk of damage, and, having set foot on a ledge, I threw my crampon on to the summit. After two or three failed attempts, its prongs hooked on to some fissure. I hauled on the end; it was solidly retained up above, and hauling myself up would be child's play for my young muscles.

Nello, sensing that he was impotent to follow me, whimpered. I attached him to my shoulders, and it did not take us long to find ourselves standing on the rump of the islet. It measured a hundred meters around, and generous life had sown a few plants there, proof against the spray: blue thistles and wild myrtles.

I stayed to watch the sun sink into the sea, covering everything, from the west to the east, with a silk part-yellow and part-violet. At times, incandescences succeeded one another in the celestial dome and the marine plain, attenuating beneath the fall of the mauve veils of dusk. Sensing the melancholy rising within me to which the effacement of a beauty always gives, I got ready to depart. I looked at my watch; it was exactly seven forty-five.

Suddenly, I saw Nello stop, his gaze fixed on the ground, his feet trembling and his fur bristling. I leaned over and I picked up from the rock a marvelous rose: a yellow rose, in all the splendor of its bloom. I considered the flower with amazement; it had been freshly cut. At the clean break in the stem, the sap was still exhaling its moisture; drops of dew were pearling on the flesh of the petals, the soft mat gold flesh of which roses share the glory with the breasts of a few very young women.

How had that beautiful flower of fecund earth come to be on that desolate rock? A rose only lives for three days, even with the care of a prodigious gardener. Even out there on the "mainland," I had never seen such a bush within a kilometer of the grim cliff. A human hand must, therefore, have let that rose fall. But how?

We were certainly not on the parquet of a ballroom, where flowers fall, still warm from inhabiting the cleavages of young women. Had some female passer-by, an audacious tourist, in the arms of an agile companion, scaled the sheer granite and sown there the gracious souvenir of a pleasant hour? Before sending my crampon up to the plateau of the island I had searched minutely for a sequence of asperities permitting the ascension of a gymnast. It was quite impossible to reach it without a ladder or a rope. Had someone had the pleasant idea of throwing the flower on to the reef from the deck of a passing boat, as a coquettish socialite might send a smile to some rude vagabond on the road? Even admitting that a boat might skirt the rock closely enough to permit the gesture, a rose is too light a projectile to be thrown to that height. A pebble, yes; a flower, no.

It was, however, not impossible that a human hand had thrown that rose on the ground, since a man had found it there. But where had it been plucked? The nearest land was four leagues distant, and it was not on a harsh rocky coast battered by all the winds that rosebushes blossom gloriously. Now, the rose had just been plucked; the freshness of its petals pearled with dew and the moistness of the break in its stem proved that irrefutably.

And I intoxicated myself inhaling the suave breath of the flower, seeking to divine the enigma of its arrival.

How stupid I am, I finally thought. *Some luxury yacht must have passed by, with a young woman aboard who takes pleasure in seeing plants flourish though the windows of a greenhouse. That's the explanation. Anyway, I'll be able to settle the matter. At the nearest sem-*

aphore, the watchman will tell me what boats have passed this way.

And while a sight inflated my adolescent breast at the thought that, far away over there, on the land—very far away from me—was a corsage that would palpitate more forcefully if my hand ornamented it with that adorable rose. I passed the flower through the buttonhole of my reefer jacket, and got ready to quit the block of granite that had offered me a charming and enigmatic souvenir.

Night was falling. The failing light was making its last effort, more potent behind the strongly contoured silhouettes of things, for it was the hour when the duel of light and shadow becomes tragic and solemn.

Nello had quit me, and was lying on a point of the rock. I tried to pick him up in order to attach him to my shoulders and descended thus along the rope, as I had climbed up; but the good dog, always so obedient, ran away. He moaned when I touched him; I was obliged to take hold of him by force.

I was heading back into port when I perceived in the twilight the pilot's boat heading out to sea. I drew alongside in order to satisfy my curiosity.

"Pilot," I asked, after the words of greeting, "have any ships passed here recently?"

"None has been seen for a long time. It's three days since a sail or smoke has been seen at the semaphore. I'm hoping for a Dundee from Bayonne, which might arrive tonight, but neither you nor I will be going home again before tomorrow; we'll have a flat calm, and the ebb-tide would be against you."

So no boat had approached the reef for three days! But in that case, it could not have been a human hand that had thrown the rose! I contemplated the rose flowering my breast. Its flesh had the velvet gleam of buds that the dawn causes to open slightly on the bush. I sensed the eight of an anxious gaze upon it, that of Nello, who, taking refuge on the stem, motionless, seemed to be prey to an inexplicable terror.

The instinct of animals foresees danger. Had Nello been warned of a squall? I interrogated the sky and the waves: no symptom.

My thought, however, toiled over the origin of the mysterious rose, and I pleased myself imagining that a seagull had brought it from the land in the tip of its bright beak, as the dove of the ark carried the olive branch.

O amorously beautiful night. The pilot had been correct to announce flat calm. The bosom of the sail was as flaccid as that of an old woman. The phosphorescent sea was as polished as mercury. The red globe of the moon, launched abruptly from behind a cliff with the surge of an incandescent balloon, rose toward the zenith trailing a golden yellow wake over the water and a vast blonde light in the sky.

Running around the *Minar* over the silver silk of the water, like marine will-o'-the-wisps were the rapid fleeting lights—charged with augural menace according to the mariners of our coast, who call them "beuliers," and also ancient navigators, who, astonished to see stars descending from the sky to frolic upon the waves in capricious couples, named them Castor and Pollux, like the twins of the zodiac, I amused myself following the meanders of those vagabond flames, the scintillating wake of which Nello accompanied with muted growls.

Abruptly, a gust of wind rived from the sea so violent that, without an instinctive thrust of the tiller, the

Minar would have capsized. Then the sea suddenly swelled. It became urgent to diminish the sail.

"Here, Nello!" I shouted "To the bar!"

Ordinarily so obedient, in such conformity with my ideas, the dog did not budge, and responded with a prolonged howl, always sinister in the night. Evidently, he was reluctant to approach me. But I had other things to do than fathom the causes of his ill humor. I succeeded in bringing in the lateen and trimming the mainsail, and the frail boat made as much headway as she could on the heavy sea, which reared up at the perpetual refusal of crazy winds coming from all directions.

Certainly, I hold in great pity the stupid conceptions of moderns who consider the forces of nature as devoid of intelligence and soul. The instinct of the people, and their immemorial traditions—which are more reliable than the hypotheses of pedants—are able to divine the mysterious entity and the personality of the spirits of the elements, which the science of the Ancients knew so profoundly. Anyone who has been in peril at sea has sensed around him the conscious design of the winds, the hostile maneuvers of some, favorable of others. That night, in the turbulence of furious winds, my intuition, although sharpened by the danger, did not perceive any breath of assistance. There was no human aid for which to hope, not one vessel in sight. I was quite alone on that ferocious sea. And between the crazy lurches of my courageous boat, I searched the horizon desperately for the gleam of lighthouses, while Nello added his lamentable howls to the racket.

Suddenly, the squall calmed down; a fresh breeze carried us to port. My eyes thought of seeking the rose in my buttonhole. It was no longer there. I could not see it in the boat.

"Seek, Nello, find the rose!"

The dog did not budge, still fearful, his fur bristling. He was growling and panting. By following the direction of his gaze I found the rose again. I felt myself go pale. In the light of the nascent morning, the rose was as fresh and as beautiful as at the moment when I had found it on the rock. The break in the stem was beginning to dry out, but the soft flesh of the petals conserved its radiant suavity. So the winds, the spray, the splashes of foam and sea-water had not been able to adulterate the freshness of that strange rose! I sensed the advent within me of I know not what distant and tenebrous horror.

In the house, a telegram had been waiting for me since the evening. I shivered before opening it. I read: *Elsa died suddenly this evening at seven forty-five.*

Seven forty-five! The precise moment when I had picked up the fatal rose on the rock. Elsa! Elsa, so full of life and beauty! My beloved Elsa! I fell unconscious.

I learned later that, all afternoon on that sinister day, she had worn a yellow rose in her corsage.

THE DAY OF THE GLORIFICATION

To Auguste Rodin

> The spirits only touch the Beautiful
> in order to produce the Beautiful.
> Shakespeare, *Measure for Measure.*[15]

The city woke up in the spring dawn.

Emerged from nocturnal repose in order to abandon itself to the unexpectedness of the new day, life stammered its first matinal rumors; a slight buzz rose up from white houses toward the dry clarity of the sky.

Already, the silhouettes of the inhabitants were crossing the public square. It would be a pleasant day to be alive in that calm city. The square, a hemicycle whose cord approached the shore, was ringed by little cubic palaces flanked by thin Corinthian pilasters supporting the entablature of terraces. At the back of the semicircle was a monopteral temple of fortunate proportions with a fronton sculpted with a chorus of Muses.

From the square one could see the entire gulf in the hollow of which the town was staged. The violently blue sea rolled its somnolent waves into the port, where the

---

[15] I have translated this quotation from the French text quoted in the original; the parallel line (from Act 1, Scene 1) in the original reads: "Spirits are not finely touched/But to fine issues."

tips of masts were visible. Along the edges of the gulf, which launched forth in two sharp horns, hills appeared, still violet under the dew vaporized by the sun. In the occident was a hill with flanks covered in myrtles, and tamarisks and flowering oleanders around its base.

In the open country, gilded soil alternates with the thickest masses of mulberries, orange-trees, cypresses and vines.

The low houses are grouped around dominating temples, like sheep clustered around their pastors. Those neglected dwellings are clearly those of men whom the clemency of the weather permits a free life under the sky, a life of leisure and sensations, exempt from effort and covetousness. One only penetrates over the thresholds in order to sleep.

The magnificence of a hieratic architecture is still reserved for the gods. The temples, of a homogeneous character but an organization varied in accordance with their consecration, enclose the marvels of an art conscious of the great symbolism that it exalts: inside, mythical frescoes of an audacious and confident coloration; outside, sculptures of a heroic grace. The entire city is strewn with statues of a sovereign beauty.

There is no vestige of barbarity, and yet no indication of softness. The city has remained half way between the two stags. One might think it a Corinth ignorant of the laxity of decadence.

The people have arrived in the public square.

It is the day of a solemn festival. On a platform to which one accedes by marble steps, the magistrates and priests will come to sit down on seats of pink porphyry whose uprights are carved into sphinxes.

That population belongs to an unusually beautiful race. Where have those beings learned that nobility of their attitudes, the rhythm of their gestures, the elegance of their gait? Certainly, a multiple heredity of beauty, corroborated by an esthetic education, has fashioned these bodies, so supple under the harmonious undulations of the draperies in which they are clad.

Men with gazes of a constant serenity are circulating and chatting. Their arms, emerging naked from red or white tunics, have a robust musculature not dishonored by any heaviness. The women pass with a eurhythmia of bearing, as in Panathenaias: courtesans whose forms are visible under subtle Ceos gauze; their loose hair caresses their unveiled breasts, and tame goats follow them like dogs; young women with delightfully carnal faces, whose smiles are ornamented with gravity for having perceived the young men imploring them for amour.

To the left, at the fountain where chimeras weep water into a white bowl, groups of maidservants are chatting while filling urns; and naked children are pestering them, exciting large svelte dogs against them.

A movement ran through the assembly. On the platform, which faced the sea, processions of men and young men arranged themselves symmetrically. They were the most honored individuals of the city: priests, poets, sculptors, painters, musicians and gymnasiarchs. The young women in peplums of white wool, with admirable tresses circled by bandlets woven with gold, were the priestesses of Aphrodite, who surrounded the statue of their divinity, soaring, with a quiver of her powerful wings, above a sphere that she was brushing with her foot.

The old sculptor Karites was seated on a tripod overlooking the crowd. The duty of presiding over the solemn festival belonged to him. After having populated his fatherland with masterpieces, Karites, sensing that age was putting a brake on his creative impetus, had refused to decline. With the serenity of a worker satisfied with the task achieved, he had thrown his chisel and his files into the sea and renounced carving marble with a hand weighted down by the years. Now Karites, appointed as the agonothetes, had the mission, with the poets, artists and priests, of watching over the normal development of human beauty in the city. He was the great conservator of the charm of the race.

Silence fell when the old man rose to his feet,

"As every year, here we are, united in accordance with the rite of the ancestors, to offer the consecration of our homages to the two highest apparitions of human glory, Genius and Beauty. Real fatherland, race quivering before the august mystery of colors and forms, collectivity exceptionally liberated from barbarity, crowd of election apt to divine, in the mythic splendor of things and beings, the scattered soul of the gods, salutations! Salutations! Today we shall enunciate what we have decided, in the untroubled serenity of our souls, we who invest consciousness with the unique power of our superior meditation.

"This is the day when, faithful to our law, we must designate the man and the woman whose appearances we want to immortalize. We must name that young woman and that young man, worthy, one by her beauty and the other by his genius, of our great sculptor Lysidias making their effigies emerge from the marble. Who, then, are those two beings, to whom we shall elevate statues?

"All year long, with a constant zeal, we, the ministers of the cult of Beauty, have visited the gymnasts, contemplated works of art, listened to hymns and read poems. We have rejoiced in seeing slender ephebes and gracious virgins, in penetrating noble works, the flowers of supreme souls. Finally, we have judged. This is the result.

"In order that her ephemeral form shall leave its imperishable and tangible memory of the earth that she ornaments, in order that her youth and her grace shall not be effaced from the earth like a fleeting charming dream, in order that her glory shall be forever sacred even to the eyes of barbaric posterities, the young woman who seems the most beautiful to us this year, will be sculpted by Lysidias. That young woman is Antheis, and here she is!"

At a gesture from Karites, two young women lift a radiant creature up on to a pedestal, in view of the people. One unfastened the bandlet snaking over the virgin's head, the other removed the two light clasps maintaining her loose robe. The garment fell at her feet, as the gilded tresses flowed down to her kidneys. Confused, her arms interlaced over her palpitating breasts, in a proud gesture full of grace, Antheis appeared in the radiation of her beauty. The priestesses threw handfuls of roses and privet flowers toward her, children with thurifers expelled a blue vapor of burnt aromatics, and the charmed crowd shouted.

Reverberated by the firmament and the sea, a silvery light caressed the young body as if natural forces and unknown gods had wanted to envelop with their mysterious tenderness that perfect work of Life, that definitive creature, the aspect of whom was consolation for so many abortive sketches. It was a triumphal moment.

Lysidias, the master sculptor, contemplated his future model with ecstatic eyes.

"This," proclaimed Karites, "is the Antheis whose form we wish to consecrate to immortality. Have we judged well?" And, parading his interrogative gaze over the people, he added: "Does anyone opposite it?"

"Me!" replied a voice.

A young man bounded on to the platform and planted himself in front of Karites.

At the sound of his voice, Antheis, shivering, had leapt down from the pedestal and veiled herself.

"Who are you, young man?" Karites demanded of the newcomer, "and on what authority do you support your pretention?"

"I am Antheis's fiancée. My right is that of amour. The beauty of that child is mine, by the force of oaths exhaled between kisses. I do not want the body in which her promised soul palpitates to be perpetual for the delights of unknown men. All of you, who have already contemplated it for an instant, only possess a foggy memory of it, a vain illusion, a vanished vision. To me alone, to me whose life is suspended on her lips, Antheis has sworn to be the living dream in the mystery of nuptial evenings. What! When she and I, a rapid couple, have disappeared from this world though which we are passing, when I shall no long longer see her, and no longer have her, the men of other centuries, contemplating the radiant image of what my Antheis was, will intoxicate their reverie with the beauty from which I shall be separated? They will see her; perhaps they will pledge the faith of their hallucinated amour to her? No, I don't want that! I want Antheis, disdainful of leaving that immortal reflection of herself, to descend entirely, on the fatal day, into one of the twin urns that receive our ashes."

A murmur rose from the crowd as the young man's words were discussed. On their seats, the old men had listened with an indulgent air. Karites exchanged a few words with his neighbor in a low voice, while smiling.

"Child," he said, "the naivety of your jealousy is not made to displease us, we who have known the fever of passions. That absolute right of which you boast over the beauty of a creature, the faith of Antheis invests you with it, but not the gods. Certainly she has a right, that privileged child, to bury the notion of her charm in the bosom of the man preferred between all. Certainly, she can attribute that gift, the memory of her young splendor, to a unique living individual. But her ineradicable duty is to make, for those who dream, this gift: a vision of her beauty. Were the gods, in creating Antheis thus, only thinking of her and of you? When we light lamps, is it therefore for themselves? What would you say, young man, to the musician who, the creator of a work consoling for noble bruised souls, burned his unrevealed music at the feet of a woman—homage or sacrilege? We will not grant your prayer, jealous child. Listen; a man is about to appear whose speech enchants breasts. Listen to him, and then tell us whether you persist in the egotism of your resolution."

Karites turned to the approving people. "It remains for us to name the man whose genius we desire to glorify. For, in order to erect a statue to some sublime individual, we do not wait for death to abolish his form; we do not wait until the years have withered his face and dishonored his limbs. Life is short; we leave to the barbarians the wait for hypothetical tomorrows. Faithful to the counsels of nature, we strive to collect, like a ripe fruit, the rapid moment; and it is the appearance of powerful and fecund youth that we want to fix in matter slow to disappear. It is at the hour when we see the harmonic development of his strength triumphant that we pay a man the tribute of our admiration.

"A poet has revealed himself among us, great and noble. For that dear blossoming, let there be a fête in the entire city, as in the intimacy of our spirits. And that is why we have decided that the chisel of Lysidias will execute the image of the poet Mylittes, in order that people to come may know the man whose poems will have given them fine hours.

"Mylittes is unknown to us; his verses were sung by the lips of friends. If he is here, let him come to us. Our virgins will place crowns on his forehead, to which our sages will summon the kiss of the stars."

A young man emerged from the crowd and presented himself. "I am the man whose verses you have loved."

The old men got up from their seats and bowed respectfully. A calm melancholy floated over his face. And piously, the young women brought him flowers, sweet for sad souls

"You have elected me, a solitary poet to whom you want to raise a statue. Now you have seen me. The honor that your intention attributes to me would be a shame for me: I am ugly."

He wept. An anxiety passed through the silent people. A woman kissed the hem of his mantle.

"Master," said Karites, "stand up straight; you do not have the right to weakness, genius."

"Alas, the urn is disgraceful that contains the perfume. The beauty about which I wax ecstatic, was not my endowment. I have meditated, a sad dreamer, beside the sonorous waves, while other young men, in the palaestras and the gymnasia pursued, smiling, the eurhythmic expansion of their proud forms. I forgot my body while my thought flew toward the infinite. And now here I am, an inharmonic man, a beautiful soul in a sad form. The young women with whom I come in contact run to other arms, more beautiful, without seeing the flame in my eyes. And if I sing them my poems of amour, they emotion that awakens in their heart palpitates over the memory of distant fiancés. However, I have never had either hatred or envy."

"Why are you lamenting?" Karites interjected. "Your share is the better one. You are the man who casts fortunate hours into existences. O consoler, happiness is to live intensities of emotions, and you give those intensities. Let us offer you the testimony of our gratitude."

"Well, let one of you accord me a mercy. For long enough, the duration of a life, I will have been subject to the dishonor of not being handsome. At least allow death to enable me to be reborn, immortally splendid, from my ashes. There are necessary and sublime lies; you know that, my peers, initiates who dissimulate profound certainties under the cajoling form of myths. Well, I ask to lie to future men. Listen to me: if there is a ephebe whose eyes have wept under the intoxication of my verses, if that one loves me, let him come forward. He will be Lysidias's model, and under the statue created in accordance with his form, inscribe my name."

An enthusiastic young man forestalled all the others; he was sovereignly handsome.

"Master," he asked of Mylittes, shivering, "do you judge me worthy of being the desired model?"

"Thank you, Brother! You are making me the greatest of sacrifices; you are depriving yourself of the glory of your beauty in order to adorn me with it. Thanks to your devotion, successive generations will have a resplendent memory of my mortal appearance."

An unknown voice rose up from the crowd.

"No one has the right to lie; no one has the right to usurp what nature has refused. You are yielding to your vanity, Mylittes!"

"Who said that? I pardon the ignorant individual. My duty is to enchant souls. This deceit thrown to generations by me, I owe them. I feel sorry for the man who does not understand the grandeur. And there cannot be any question here of vanity, a pettiness unknown to those who possess sacred pride, A missionary of the Word, I owe all my efforts, in order to ensure that in me, humble, the gods speaking through my lips will be respected."

Antheis, the virgin of beauty, approached; she placed her light hand on the poet's shoulder. A tear rolled down Mylittes' cheek. Antheis drank it in a kiss.

"Holy couple," cried Karites, "You, Beauty, and you, Genius, incarnate the two entities closest to the gods. We decree immortality to the hour of your youthful energy. Go in the legitimate pride of your glory! Your grace, expressed in marble, will be admired, yours, Antheis, in accordance with the truth, yours Mylittes, by virtue of a necessary lie corrective of an error of nature. And before your statue of a radiant man, poet, young women will dream of the dreamer whose form was so beautiful, as beautiful as his soul. We who create ideality have the right and the duty to recreate beings such as they ought to appear. Nature forgot to give you temporary beauty; we will give it to you immortally. Our lie is divine."

He fell silent. In the distance, the waves sang under the scented breeze, and the heavens had an immense smile of mystery. Nature continued her movement, perhaps indifferent to the two masterpieces to which she had given birth, and which humans were glorifying.

And Mylittes thought, in a sharp moment, that she threw, with a constant force, unsuspected seeds into the womb of forms...

Antheis sensed a melancholy fluttering over her smile...

They looked at one another, anxiously...

They had the consciousness of *being alive*.

THE DEATH OF LOVERS

To Maxime Maufra[16]

As each of the young women present had made her comment about the fatal end of all amour, a melancholy comment revealing old memories, Jean Songère, who had listened in silence until then, let fall these words:

"There is only one beautiful denouement for amour."

"What?" asked several voices.

"A mysterious death that carries off the two enlaced lovers. Hazard enabled me to witness, or very nearly, a death that arrived thus, sealed with a kiss."

He was summoned to relate the adventure, and commenced:

Daoulas, the painter of powerful landscapes whom you admire, had taken me to Scotland, where he wanted to paint the great emerald mountains that are surrounded by supernatural lines in the light of dawn and evening. We had decided to spend some time in a little sea port, around which Daoulas had found harsh and wild locations appropriate to his audacious art. That coast of high blue-tinted cliffs, cut by sharp zigzags, bristling with

---

[16] Maxime Maufra (1861-1918), who was born, like Michelet, in Nantes, became a noted landscape painter, particularly of Bretagne.

terrible reefs—which is as sinisterly beautiful in calm weather as in a tempest—had enthused him.

It is very dangerous, and the perfidious submarine rocks that are scattered in the region are not content to create eddies always white with foam; each of them can count the boats that they have disemboweled over the centuries.

We had hired a little pleasure boat, the *Daisy*, an agile and ardent sloop constructed for racing with such precision that a single man could have it in hand as a groom maintained a well-trained horse. In that boat we explored the blue granite indentations of the coast, and from time to time, Daoulas took out his sketch-pad, and rapidly, with violent thrusts of the pencil, made the notes necessary for future paintings.

"Tomorrow, if you wish," he said, one day, "We'll go to the Iron Islands."

The Iron Islands are an archipelago of rocks abut twenty miles from the coast.

The following day, we disembarked on Saint Patrick's Isle, the largest of those islands, which is a full two kilometers around and is the only one inhabited, by a population rising to six persons. Daoulas had brought his rifle, and we explored the islet. We arrived at a series of little beaches enclosed in coves. Rounding a corner of rock, I saw a spectacle that made me turn back in order to recommend silence to my companion who was walking behind me. He was preparing to fire at an imprudent curlew unused to encountering humans in its domain. I lifted up the barrel of the weapon urgently.

"No noise," I said. "Look!"

The hour was placidly beautiful. A short distance away, in the blue water, so limpid that we could see the dark blue feet of plunging rocks, two beautiful naked creatures were swimming in convoy, a young man and a young woman.

From the hole in the granite into which we had slid, we could not distinguish their facial features. We admired their beauty, of a rhythm so perfectly in harmony with the simple splendor of the décor.

One might have thought that the smile of that summer morning, rejoicing that grim corner of nature, of which it seemed that the tempest ought to be the fatal accompanist, had only been put on to illustrate the grace of those two beings, as gracious as youth and amour.

The head of the young woman, helmeted in pale gold, drew away from and then drew closer to the brown head of her lover, like two halcyons playing over calm water. The beauty of the human skin tone visible under the glaucous water, the beauty that makes one of the mysterious attractions lent by legend to sirens, was a fortunate complement to the beauty of the landscape, and the two young people, naked and simple, amid the sea and the rocks, represented humankind in all its strength, in the fullness of amour.

In time, the couple of swimmers resumed their footing and emerged from the water, approaching our hiding place unhurriedly. Their forms were as noble as their attitudes. Daoulas, marveling, made a sketch of the scene. We were certainly well-hidden by the spur of rock that sheltered us, but I thought I discerned, after a glance in our direction, a sudden movement of embarrassment on the part of the blonde bather. Then the disposition of the terrain hid her and her companion from our charmed eyes.

Saint Patrick's Isle possessed six inhabitants. A household of farmers cultivated a few meters of arid land there, and occupied a small house with a low roof, against which leaned the only tree on the island, a fig tree pushed there under the warm breath of a marine current. Their children spent their days playing with a cow and two goats.

The other two indigenes were innkeepers. It seemed bizarre to find an inn on that savage rock. Of the couple who maintained the hostel, the husband was charged with watching over an enormous water-enclosure constructed by a fishmonger in order to keep lobsters. The coastal fishermen often came to bring their catch to the pond, or simply found a small haven in the rocky archipelago in which to take refuge when surprised at sea by bad weather. The refuge of the men was the good inn, where, while the tempest howled, they recovered from a glass of liquor the joyful energy that struggles against fatigue and danger.

The landlady of the inn, a sprightly little red-haired woman, still young, cooked us a few fish and we sat down for lunch. Soon, the young man and the young woman we had surprised bathing came into the room. On seeing us they had the movement of annoyance of two beings whose habitual solitude is being violated. But they put on a brave face against fortune and sat down at the small table that was waiting for them.

I thought I had seen, at the sight of us, a fugitive blush invade the cheeks of the young woman. Now I could see her profile, and I was able to appreciate the details of her beauty.

She gave an impression of gilded blondeness. The ringlets that curled around her forehead, and the brightness of her youthful complexion, seemed to exhale a blonde light around her delicate and tender face, in which the blue-green eyes concentrated the life. She was a truly delightful creature, whose slender and lively gestures revealed suppleness and strength.

Her companion, in whom I immediately recognized a Frenchman, had not attained thirty. His garments did not attenuate the character of strength that his body showed. He was grave, with a constant pallor.

Without paying any attention to us, the amorous couple chatted in low voices. It seemed to me that a sad shadow wandered over their solitary happiness.

When they had gone, the loquacious landlady, compensating herself for the forced silence to which her sojourn on a desert island often condemned her, recounted everything she knew about her two guests. The young woman was American. I had suspected as much from her accent and the energy of gesture that the daughters of North America have. The young man was French. They had come to visit the island one day as tourists, and, the abode pleasing them, they had resolved to spend some time there.

They had been living there for three months, far from society, which they seemed to have forgotten completely. They gave themselves entirely to their amour, indifferent to any other thought and any other dream. They had the custom of making excursions on the sea, alone in a little boat, in which they had landed there. The fishermen who chanced to encounter them in the course of events followed the gracious couple, radiant with amour, with an indulgent eye.

Several times, in our excursions, we too crossed the path of the little boat in which the two young people were locked in an embrace.

One night, Daoulas and I were still some distance from our port. The breeze had dropped, there was not a breath in the flaccid sail.

"What forces us to return to land?" I said to Daoulas, who had taken the oars. "Let's take advantage instead of seeing this admirable night for longer."

In fact, the spectacle was magical. The moon filled the light atmosphere with bright silver. As is often the case after a hot day, the sea was phosphorescent. Our sloop, scarcely advancing at the whim of the current, designed a wake of diamonds in the circle of water of which we were the center, a circle of sea-water deadened by immobility, but with a passionately vibrant splendor. A pearly flutter agitated around us; every drop of stirred water was a spark, and myriads of gleams scattered at every stroke of the oar. Only the ruddy glow of distant lighthouses reminded me that the land exited, and the life—the hard life—of humans.

"Look!" exclaimed Daoulas. "There are the lovers of the Iron Islands."

"Nothing more is lacking to this night," I said, "for some god has made it for two beings who love one another. Let's ply the oars as gently as possible and go past them."

Soon, we found ourselves abreast of the little cutter, with was almost motionless. It was gliding toward us under the wind, and, dissimulated by our sail, we could see the gracious lovers at our leisure. They were enlaced at the foot of the mast; their elegant silhouettes stood out vigorously against the silvery light. The young woman had tilted back the nape of her neck on her lover's bosom, and the gilded halo that her blonde beauty exhaled became more intense amid the pearly gleam of the night.

The young man had abandoned the tiller, and I thought I remarked a rope around the waists of the beautiful enlaced couple, tying them together. Why?

"Hey, Monsieur!" shouted Daoulas's voice, breaking the charm of the silence, "take hold of your bar. There are perfidious currents here that will take you straight toward a reef!"

There was no response from the cutter, and we continued our route. Did those bold lovers hold men in disdain, as they held death? For a long time we were able to follow with our eyes the slender silhouette of their radiant boat, a bright shadow in the nacreous sea. What was carrying it, then, gliding with the silent majesty of a gray swan? Glad amour, amour strong enough to kill any memory stranger to itself, whether that memory was regret or remorse? First amour, ingenuous or definitive, or amour disturbed by a menace more precise than the ordinary one of destiny?

Gradually, the little cutter charged with that beautiful burden was effaced by the blurred clarities of our horizon.

A few days later, we learned that the cadavers of two young people had been found on the coast, bound together by a rope.

On the night when we had encountered them, a customs officer had perceived their cutter drifting toward a place strewn with rocks. He had shouted with all his might and fired rifle shots in order to attract the attention of the imprudent individuals. Nothing had budged in the boat, which had sunk before the customs officer's eyes. The eddies had swallowed that amour and protected its mystery.

Had those two beings slid toward death unconsciously or voluntarily, or simply indifferent to the state of life or death?

Their names were unknown. The innkeeper on Saint Patrick's Isle knew no more about her guests than she had told us.

When, in the presence of families of mariners who had come piously, the gravedigger had thrown the last spadeful of earth on the bier in which the inseparable couple reposed, we scattered coastal flowers, sea-pinks and immortelles, over the disturbed earth, and on the anonymous cross I wrote these simple words:

Passer-by, if you have loved, pray here for two beings who died loving one another.

INCANTATION BY THE TEN DIVINE NAMES

To Edmond Haraucourt

Ain Soph! Mantle of night that no eye contemplated, threshold of shadow on which Apollonius and Moses were exhausted, wearied by having broken down the previous forty-nine doors! One day, dazzled by glory, we shall penetrate into your abyss with the confidence of approaching the shores off the fatherland. Let the vertigo of traveling toward you, by paths of pain, attract our loins, bruised by effort and wounded by darts! Essence of all things, who crowns with eternity the hours of time, with infinity the zones of space and the multiplicities of number, whatever my intoxication might be in having suspected your mystery, I shall not blaspheme to the extent of projecting my vain human voice toward your silence. I know that you are too far away from me, O primordial modality of Being, you of whom the differentiation, source of my life and source of universal evil, was perhaps no more—and here lie the limits of terror!—than an immemorial accident, But by the ten beams of light that your central shadow projects, by the ten conductors of your vibrations, by the ten delegates of your Amour, I summon the virtues of your principal emanations. Organs of a body of which you are the invisible heart, I want each of them to quiver at my voice and respond by an effusion of its energies toward my bosom.

My strength commands them and my weakness implores them.

I

Eheie![17] The eye has never seen your simple majesty enthroned in the Empyrean, nor, in your long face circled by a crown of lightning, your mouth, which orders the Holy Animals to undertake vertiginous courses into the utmost depths of the first cause, and proffers the significant names of things. I want the Prince with the faces of serenity to introduce before your shadowed face the multicolored procession of my violent desires, which will climb, toward you, accursed and flagellated, the nine steps of the ladder of the heavens.

II

Iah! My poetic imagination, humanizing the mirage of your essence and nestling in the shell of Space, glimpses the gesture of your hands in a night populated by stars beyond the orbit of the planets of which our sun is the center. The races of which I am the issue believed that they saw your reflection in the mild eyes of a man with red hair who, born in a stable between an ox and an ass, was nailed to a cross; and women adore your pale reflection around the bloody head of that young man. Your bosom clad in Wisdom emerges from the seed of a father. Let your hands, occupied in juggling with the Wheels, with the spheres symbolizing your ideas, re-

---

[17] Hebrew, signifying "I am." In company with the other names, with slightly different spellings it can be found in chapter IV of Francis Barrett's guide to Cabalistic Magic.

dress with lucidity the troubles of my eyes! The human spirit easily sinks into chaos. Let Raziel, your confident genius, make his voice heard in the burning bush that tints my desires with a reflection of flame.

III

JodHeVauHe![18] I have seen on the horizon a ray of sunlight illuminate with a yellow redness the white underside of the dove, encrusting in the heavens, by the perpendicularity of its deployed wings, the appearance of a cross. Thus you luster manifest life with a vibration of your intelligence. From your bosom, great and strong Angels go to invest the old man Saturn with the power to command creation and the effacement of forms. In a black hood constellated with garnets, forehead diademed with sad lead, here I am, burning sulfur flowers in order that you might carry me away in spirit. O azure smoke, to the supreme limits of the sidereal domain, to the border of the empyrean world. You will guide me, Zaphiel, into the darkness of the Mystery in which my audacity will be engulfed, and you will envelop me with immortality, in spite of the sinister demon Zazel, who sniggers at soon conducting my form and by blood to decrepitude, and then to definitive putrescence.

IV

El![19] The scepter with three branches in your right hand, and the index finger rigid like a juvenile phallus, it is you that Orpheus distinguishes on the summit of

---

[18] The tetragrammaton often rendered as Jehovah.

[19] A syllable meaning "God" in various Semitic languages.

Olympus, magnificent and merciful, projecting the luminous swarm of the Dominations toward the sphere of Jupiter. The wood of aloes and nutmeg consumed in cassolettes cloud with their smoke my forehead circled with bronze, my limbs at ease beneath the bright blue robe dotted with topazes. You bring me the scepter, Zadkiel, the baton of command. Inaccessible to the suggestion of Hismael, I shall only brandish it in the name of justice and adorable mercy.

V

Elohim Ghibor![20] For the gods also, like humans and the planetary genii, have a body sculpted in the beauty of matter. In your yellow flesh flows a marvelous blood, O dispenser of force! Father of heroic hearts, at the kiss of the Powers that you delegate, Mars recovers strength for the struggle. Here: helmeted with steel, in a poppy-red robe inflamed by a scintillation of rubies, the vapors of storax dilate my nostrils. Samael, archangel whose robust chin one glimpses in the abrupt glints of the sword, you will pour the oil of your strength on my loins girdled in leather, and you will give aggressive energy and resistance for the perpetual combat of living, for holy revolt and just wrath. And against Barbazel, the violent demon of brutality, hatred and ravage, I will extend the point of the consecrated blade.

---

[20] "Mighty God," responsible for chastisement.

VI

Eloha![21] You meditate the luminous dream of beauty. On the wings of Kings of the Splendor your gaze arrives through the vital furnace of the sun all the way to the forehead of the poet haloed with gold. Among the radial choir of Apollonides, O Beauty, I was born to adore your face! The golden tiara with three stages on my hair, in a cope of orphrey ocellated with carbuncles, now I am throwing tears of mastic and laurel flowers on to the ardent embers. Taphael or Phobos, O prince of glory, you will fill my bosom with the joy of being in the world. From the sensual quiver before the grace of forms and the seduction of colors to the ecstasy taking flight toward intangible entelechies, I ascend in your wake toward the summit where absolute beauty is resplendent. Beauty, what brute has called you perishable? Your untarnishable essence, like your mortal appearance, Light, which procreates them, propagates their reflections in the sphere of eternity. For the eyes of seers, there is no extinct splendor. I implore you, Sorath!

VII

Iodevauhe Tsebaoth![22] It is by victory that you are manifest, by the victory of life over death. Your seed stimulates the Elohim toward the smiling sphere of Ve-

---

[21] A slightly different version of the name of God employed in V

[22] A version of the tetragrammaton Yod-He-Vau-He slightly different from the one given in II, with the addition of a word meaning "Hosts", i.e. "God of Hosts." VIII is etymologically identical

nus, genetrix of amour. In a celadon simarre speckled with emeralds, temples clasped by a copper-red coronet florid with vervain and roses, intoxicated by the effluences of musk and saffron, I invoke you, Anael, in the hour when your planetary body comes to charm with its beauty the Bull of the Zodiac. The violent ecstasy of amour carrying the soul outside life, to the edge of death—for to possess an ideal is to modify the form of one's life as profoundly as death—ecstasy of amour, you can pour from the cup that your charming hand holds. The lover who was destined for me, before the earth, the lost half of the androgyne that I was, you will send toward my kiss. Prevent, I beg you, the queens of the stryges, Lilith and Nahemah, from holding her captive in the unknown night. Put into the womb of the beloved woman the vibration of amour that will be perpetuated, through the marrow of the Elohim, all the way to the very heart of God. And neutralize with your embalming breath the malevolent spells of the demon jealous of beautiful happy couples, Anteros or Kademel.

VIII

Elohim Tsebaoth! On the left-hand column you stand in a nimbus of glory, and from there your servants, the sons of the gods, soar toward the agile planet Mercury. On the nape of my neck a crown of hydrargyrum reposes; I have donned the mauve tunic dotted with crystal, from which my laborer's arms emerge naked. In a smoke of juniper and cinnamon, here you are, Michael, you who advised Solomon, the king of the Mystery! By means of you I want the penetration of the hidden springs, I want to fabricate the key that violates the locks of the Occult. You will not trouble, Taphthartharath, the good workman bent over the task.

IX

Shadai![23] Your feet are supported on the Fundament and your fingers make the signs to the ministers of Fire who follow the course of the Moon around our Earth. I have placed in my hair a slender silver crescent; draped in a white fluted dalmatic stared with argyroliths and sapphires, I am burning myrrh while proffering the words that force wills. You lean toward me, Gabriel, like triform Artemis at the appeal of Endymion. Soul of the Moon, your gaze invests with a guardian angel each of the children of woman, and pours the somber fire of genius into predestined breasts; your respiration enables us to believe, your aspiration to perish, and the odor of your breath attracts, through the horror of auric torrents, the spirits of the dead that we love, the imagination of poets and omen. Mirror that reflects on our foreheads the rays coming from all the planes of the abyss, choose amorously those that you project toward my loins. At the frisson of the incantation, prolonged in spiritual waves, abandon, I command you, the indifference of your frequent neutrality, in order that, alive, my seer's gaze might be launched beyond your domain. And when you touch me with the kiss of benevolent death, I will not be rolled by the astral torments, prey to the infernal em-

---

[23] Yet again, simply "God," but often translated as "Almighty God", although it is often used nowadays as a girl's name. The adjective *aourique*, which I have transcribed as "auric," seems to be idiosyncratic to Michelet.

brace of the servants of Hasmodai, the Lemurs and the Larvae.

X

Adonai Melech![24] You have realized it, the unfathomable dream of the Long Visage, which the eye has not seen! The distant crowned Macroprosopus, you have established on the realm of forms, which it harasses with the whip of perpetual Becoming. Great Architect venerated by masons, you have constructed the Temple. Since our work, Being can mirror itself in the symbol that manifest its virtualities. The shadow has a body. Great Pan is alive. At your command, the Intelligences of glory offer to the Masters among men the wine of Knowledge, the integral Gnosis, which only the strong and the audacious can savor. I know that its taste is bitter and mortal, but I can pose my lip on the cup, for in the subterrain of Eleusis I have eaten the drum and drunk the symbol.

---

[24] Adonai, yet again, means "God," Melech means "King."

HOLWENNIOUL

If your ideal is mortal, you will die of
attaining it. If your ideal is immortal, you
will become immortal for attaining it.

The sun was setting over the calm sea.

Already, an inferior segment of its disk, with the
redness of hot metal, had disappeared, sunk beneath the
horizon undulant with waves, while around the rest of
the circumference, vapors were accumulating, scarcely
less ardent than the star itself, as if basking in the secondary pride of being the reflections of a splendor.

From the bay, the displayed surface, which seemed
to follow an almost insensible upward inclination toward
the sunset, developed in an immense azure carpet in
which the caprices of color gave birth to light waves
tinted golden yellow on their vacillating crests.

To the left, the isle of Seizhun, flat and low to the
extent of brushing sea-level like an elliptical raft, inter-
rupted the unity of the sheet, and all around it, thousands
of scattered reefs, only one side of which was illuminated by the horizontal rays, were then enormous flowers of
flame inclining their black calices toward the eastern
land, and the currents between them glistened like steel
serpents.

The bay, open in a crescent, was terminated to the
left by a sharp point of gigantic rocks, at the foot of
which perpetually furious waves were breaking with a

muted din and swirls of foam were splashing the summit of the cape, a hundred times the height of a man above.

The beach of Anaoun was there, behind which the ground was scored with ravines between two sheer rocky elevations: the beach whose sand was so white that it was said to be made of the bones of the dead cast up by the waves; here and there, the fragments of skeletons could still be seen, deposited by the high tide. But the sandy relays with the ivory reflections and the harsh soil strewn with couch-grass and immortelles disappeared then, trampled by a multitude.

There were men with long hair and muscular torsos, girdled with strips of leather, old men whose goatskin cloaks hid backs that were still robust, and women ornamented as on days of festival with necklaces of multi-colored glass. From the level of the heads emerged the figures of horsemen, whose helmets surmounted with bronze wings or metallic mouths of animals scintillated under the play of the light. Between the groups, immobilized by waiting, naked children were running around with a fearful joy, mingling with short-haired dogs. The crowd, agitated by an anxious tremor, only spread in the atmosphere a noise equal to that of the waves.

All gazes converged on the horizon, and beyond the successive waves, arriving at eye-height in order to collapse on the shore, they were fixed on a dozen boats moving between the land and the island, between the disseminated reefs. They were coming under the impulsion of a gentle breeze blowing from the cape over the bay. In spite of the calm, however, the crossing, furrowed by eddies, could only be achieved by mariners of supreme skill.

The boats were nevertheless advancing with ease, cradled by the blue and pink undulation, and their sails dyed with crimson by the occidental light were reminiscent of the wings of swans deployed amid flames. Soon they were recognizable for the crowd. Their crews were composed uniquely of women, whose supple movements in the maneuvers attested a forceful youth.

One of the boats was two oar-lengths in advance of the flotilla, which seemed to be forming a deferential cortege, and from the land one could distinguish, bobbing up and down in accordance with the rhythm of the elegant waves, the emblematic head of a bronze ram fitted to the bowsprit.

When it was close enough to the beach for its keel to touch the bottom, the female crew, all clad in white, threw the anchor and brought in the sails. But while the naked arms hastened to slacken the strident halyards, a single female silhouette remained immobile against the mizzen mast.

Two pairs of young women jumped into the sea, found their footing and then, receiving an oval shield from their companions, raised it in their tensed arms above their heads, against the side of the boat. The woman who had thus far been following her reverie under the brightness of the sail having taken her place of the convexity of the platform offered to her feet, the four sailors began to traverse the waves, marching toward the shore, sufficiently robust to support their beautiful and impassive burden with one arm each..

Suddenly, on the land, a cry emerged from all breasts: "Holwennioul!"

And the vast voice of the multitude trembled with passionate emotion.

Meanwhile, the flotilla anchored, all the newcomers dived overboard and swam, some two hundred meters behind that mysterious leader, who seemed to be their sovereign.

Thus the High Priestess Holwennioul quit the sacred Isle of the Seven Slumbers in order to set foot on the continental soil.

The sculpted shield now unshaken by the slight oscillations of their march, the four living caryatids of her pedestal advanced slowly. In its retreats, the alternate ebb and flow of the high waves uncovered their naked torsos all the way to the broad hips circled by white loincloths, casting subtle adornments of flecks of foam and pearls of heavy water on to their loose hair and the inclination of their proud breasts.

Holwennioul was tall in stature. Carried reliably, her equilibrium confirmed by the shaft surmounted by the silvery head of a symbolic ram on which her right hand learned, she stood out, marmoreal and hieratic, against the yellow glory of the solar disk.

A mysterious charm emanated from the young woman. The leonine calm of her bronzed eyes attested a soul that no longer had any appetency to interrogate life, since it knew all the arcana, and the irrefutable grace of her gestures revealed a woman accustomed to supremacy. She had the appearance of an allegorical creature of a superhuman humanity. Her dark hair dressed her, from the nape of the neck to the ankles, with a mantle beneath which floated, in light pleats, a white robe girdled with gold. Around her temples snaked a crowd of submarine flowers with pentagonal red corollas, scintillating like rubies. One might have thought that amorous hands, despairing of collecting stars to magnify that splendid forehead, had gone to search the depths of the sea for an adornment. Over the amber flesh of her cleavage and her arms an imperious and melancholy perfume took flight. A multiple heredity of psychic elevation was legible in the broad root of the nose, in the groove surmounting the upper lip, rebellious against the vertigo of the kiss, and in the chin affirmative of a will that nothing alarms.

Was that beauty the auxiliary of Death or Life? She gave the impression of a golden flower blooming on the edge of an abyss. Innumerable impulses of amour and desire had doubtless collided with it, and pale young men must have disappeared from the earth while exalting in their inert pupils the memory of that vision.

And all the energy of those defunct adorations was concentrated in the occult world of forces, to forge for that creature a formidable magnetic armor, capable of reflecting amour as a mirror reflects an ardent solar ray on a point of shadow. Men and women quivered at the scintillation of a glimmer between her heavy eyelashes, at the flight of a smile between her young lips.

When they emerged from the waves the porters knelt down in order to bring their sacred burden closer to the ground. Holwennioul leapt from the shield on to the sand. Then, a broad-shouldered young man bounded recklessly through the crowd and fell at the feet of the newcomer.

"I love you!" he said.

The crowd vibrated and clamored. Its members sensed that an act of sacrilege had just been committed, by the unavowed intimacy of its wingless and jealous passion for a woman placed by destiny in an inaccessible sphere. A furious rush encircled the young unknown, whose robust vitality had been annihilated by a sudden intensity of emotion, and who lay unconscious. Men raised their arms against him, with iron in their hands.

Holwennioul placed her foot on the body gently, and swept away the assailants with a gesture. And while the crowd quivered again and growled like a beast from which a tamer has snatched away its prey, the young woman contemplated the inanimate audacious man silently.

Doubtless that juvenile beauty charmed her; her eyes forgot themselves in the gleam of a smile. Then, as if returning from the profundities of her thought, she shook her head with a movement that caused all her hair to undulate and extended her right hand toward the recumbent body, in a sort of distant but powerful caress.

Under the influence of that hand, after a temporary frisson, the young man fell back into a heavy immobility. Holwennioul indicated him with a finger to her women, who deposited him on a shield and loaded him on to their shoulders.

A chariot hitched to two oxen and surmounted by a light wicker throne awaited the will of the person that it was to carry away. Holwennioul climbed into it.

The crowd massed behind, still drawn toward that woman by the force of a fatal idolatry, and the cortege marched toward the nearby town, the roofs of which were bathed in the mauve mist of the falling dusk.

The slow pace of the oxen, in spite of the jolts of the wheels on the stones of the road and the shaking of the chariot, did not trouble the meditation of the beautiful creature, who, extended in an attitude denuded of pride, paraded over the surrounding things, and the slumbering forests, the gaze of her somber pupils, accustomed to seeing the invisible.

Before Holwennioul was conceived in the womb of a woman, the course of her future life had been determined.

Her mother was a virgin twenty years of age when she was summoned to the temple, at the hour when the new moon appeared in the heavens.

When, in their young evenings of joy, she and her companions celebrated in dances, clamors and laughter the expansive power of their adolescence, the sudden silhouette of the legendary edifice on the wooded horizon had often chilled their gaiety. It was, therefore, with an infinite terror that she followed through the dark meanders of a subterranean tunnel the old woman changed with conducting her.

When she returned to her customary dwelling at dawn, she was no longer the same. A cloud of anguish and joy floated over her forehead. She always refused to questions about what he had seen during that unknown night. Later, to the sole possessor of her beauty, she revealed between two kisses the memory she retained of that interval, like a strange dream.

She had arrived in a vast hall, open to the sky, azured by odorous fumes, from which symmetrically disposed columns emerged, and colossal statues of imaginary animals deployed granite wings, the shadows of which stretched out immeasurably in the yellow lamplight. Of that vision, perceived in the trouble of her senses, one detail haunted the memory of her eyes: suspended from the walls were garlands of wormwood, moonflowers and yellow ranunculus.

There were men and women there, all with sacerdotal miters on their heads, As soon as she entered, a tall old man whose gaze and movements affirmed the energy of a perpetuated youth had come toward her and welcomed her with these words:

"We salute you, virgin, in the glory of your future maternity. The stars have chosen you among women to give birth to a sublime daughter. And that is why we, who know destiny, are summoning the benedictions of the invisible world upon your womb, the imminent tabernacle of a soul of light."

That old man was tall and pale. He wore a white robe spangled with silver, on which a triple necklace of pearls and gems was displayed. His head was coiffed with a tiara covered with yellow silk, over which ran bizarre silver designs. He made a sign to a group of women, who took possession of the young woman, stripped her of her garments and laid her down naked, her arms crossed, on a granite altar engraved with unknown characters, at the four corners of which emerged the four statues of a man, a bull, a lion and an eagle.

Soon the poor girl found herself surrounded by the old man and six other men clad in different colors: one robe was the color of blood, another green, one scarlet, one sky blue, one brown and one purple. Those men, who were carrying swords, and the ceremonial dress, all rapidly glimpsed, gave her a moment of horror, during which she thought that she was consecrated to some supreme sacrifice; she closed her eyes, ready to faint; but in a very soft voice the old man reassured her.

"Don't tremble, child. Those swords, which frightened you, we have not drawn from their scabbards in order to do you harm, but in order to protect you. By the virtue of their points, our communicating wills hope to defeat the toxic influences that might weigh upon you or on the child in your womb.

Then commenced the prayers and the chants, intoned by the entire assembly, both men and women. The voices rose up solemnly, with the spirit of perfumes, toward the moon. Their tone rose from supplication to command, and the fragrance of the aromas varied in accordance with a progression analogous to that of the voices, as if some very savant will had contrived an alliance of the rhythm of the odors with the rhythm of the sounds, in order to multiply the power of one by the other.

Still lying on the altar, the young woman sensed the terror vanishing, to give way to an exceptional delight. It seemed to be penetrating her far from that room, in would unbounded by beings and things, the existence and forms of which she distinguished imperfectly, while, simultaneously, an unusual hyperacuity of her senses permitted her an extraordinarily precise perception of what was happening around her. After the disappearance of that temporary faculty, however, her memory only conserved a confused vision of that hour.

In the quivering silence that succeeded the sonorities of the prayers, the tall old man in the white robe spangled with silver approached her, holding his sword aloft. To the four corners of the room he threw successively, pronouncing each time formulae in an unknown language, water, earth and flame, which were presented to him in cups. From the fourth, empty cup he appeared to take a handful of air to throw it far away from him. The six men gathered at his sides imitated him with gestures of the sword.

Reflecting the yellow torchlight, the steel of the seven blades seemed to multiply flashes of lightning in the mist of the odorous smoke.

Then the seven individuals, one after another, pronounced words, and with the tips of their swords they traces signs on the belly of the supine child. To the appeal of their calm voices, however, she thought that she saw, in an unknowable world, among the evolving host of possibilities, the splendid form of a woman aureoled with gold respond and approach; and the rapid intuition went through her that the form in question would one day emerged, diminished as a child, from her maternal flesh.

It was the predicted infant.

From that night on, a crucible in which her soul was transmuted, the virgin carried constantly upon her flesh a silver talisman engraved with illegible signs.

Some time afterwards, a young stranger appeared in the country. As soon as she saw him, the vertigo of love caused the young woman's eyelids to flutter. From that union Holwennioul was born, and later, her sister Hennida.

Night had fallen when Holwennioul and her cortege arrived at the gates of the town. At the stir of a western breeze, while the earth was enveloped by the slate-gray velvet of the skies, the young woman had thrown a fur mantle over her shoulders, and that rare silhouette bathed in starlight, and that entire caravan, occasionally astonished one of the only watchers of the region, owls or wildcats, which mewled and fled.

The approach of galloping hooves was heard.

Soon, the form of a young and supple woman mounted on a little horse appeared, who marched straight toward Holwennioul.

"My sister!"

"Hennida!"

After kisses, Holwennioul turned to her retinue. "A horse!"

She leapt into the saddle, and the two women rode side by side, Holwennioul having put her arm around the sororal waist.

At the entrance to the town, as Hennida was looking curiously at the groups, she perceived the young man who had fallen unconscious at Holwennioul's feet lying in a cart, with the appearance of a mortuary slumber. She uttered a cry.

Her sister, who penetrated her pallor and sudden weakness, lifted her out of the saddle with a powerful effort of her arm, and sat her down in front of her on the neck of her horse. That maternal gesture revealed a robust and calm tenderness enshrouded in the heart of that creature, from whom sensibility appeared to have flown away with dreams toward unknown skies.

The next day, Holwennioul, in a light morning, caressed her sister's soul with her speech. Hennida was eighteen years old. She was a creature of grace. On seeing the two young women walking in the garden, with their arms liked, brushing the gladioli and the irises with their robes, a passer-by dazzled by the double apparition would have divined that the same blood nourished their beauty. There was a disquieting resemblance between their different individualities. They were the noon and midnight of the same day. If the mysterious splendor of Holwennioul gave birth to a starlight, the youth of Hennida was a solar radiation. One had all the charms of strength, the other the seduction of fragility. Doubtless, wearied by the noble effort of having produced the elder, nature had created the second as a light and precious work that the impact of one bad day might be sufficient to break. The solar influence had gilded the child in her tresses, in the speckling of her irises and the citrine velvet of her flesh.

They were sitting side by side on the stump of a plane tree. Holwennioul. supporting the slim torso of her sister with one arm, enveloped her face with a gaze attenuated by the veil of eyelashes; by that alone she knew what sadness filled her soul.

"Hennida," she said, smoothing the child's curls, "the wing of amour has already wounded you. Oh, I have feared so much for your dear breast the irruption of amour. Beings of our elevation, when amour comes to them, if they allow it to touch them, they die of it. Alas, you were not clad, like me, in armor proof against the passions. But I do not want to see a shadow pass over your brightness, O living smile. Recount your heart to me. In the lilt of your beloved voice I will forget my cares."

"Oh," sighed Hennida, putting her arms around her sister's powerful neck, "if he doesn't love me, I shall die of despair. You, who know the art of charming, be my aid. You, who command the thunder, are able to order souls. As you expelled the fever from my infantile bosom, expel suffering today, and as you give me health, give me happiness."

"Oh, if happiness were the mantle that covers my shoulders, how quickly I would take it off in order to wrap you in it!"

"Do people not whisper marvelous stories of our power? Can you not, by directing into the world of forces the incantations and prayers of the magical virgins of whom you are the sovereign, cause the influx of the planets to descend wherever you wish? Do you not have for a slave, O sacred virgin, the royal trinity: Science, Will and Sanctity? The world is a serpent whose head you trample underfoot. Why, then can you not surround with a radiant aureole of joy the forehead of a humble child, your sister?"

"How many human beings have uttered your young cry toward happiness? Since no palpitation of a heart, whoever it might be, leaves me indifferent, could I see your emotion without shivering from head to toe? The gods themselves cannot invest a human creature with happiness. In order for that to be the case, it would be necessary that a unanimous felicity englobing the earth unfurled at their feet like a harmonious sea. A law forbids constant happiness to fill a human heart as long as there are tears and suffering somewhere. O dear, pure head that that I would like so much to be happy, you are suffering the repercussion of human misery."

"And if life is an obstacle to happiness, deliver me from it. That you can do."

"You, you are requesting the somber refuge of death! There are beings who, more than others, need happiness. Your flesh, favorite gilded by the sun, would etiolate quickly in shadow. In the suffering where the grim soul of martyrs blossoms, you would wither, flower of light and joy."

"The amorous eyes of the beloved are the suns far from which my forehead is languishing. Oh, if I were in the circle of his arms, I sense that I could only emerge from it to penetrate into death. If the unknown delight came to me of which I caress desperately the fugitive hope, might I be delivered forever from living hours that would not be equal to that one! How do other women resign themselves still to suffer existence after having known such instants?"

"It is because they were not born for the unique amour. It is because, in its seed, their will received an impulsion toward other desires; it is because the energy of their being is not concentrated toward a single ideal. You, my sweet passionate sister, think that nothing except amour is worthy to occupy the sanctuary of your soul. Since it has been given to you to encounter your master, the man with whom your womanhood must fuse to constitute the definitive unity of being, your destiny is enviable. How many have languished until the final hour, whose sad eyes have never seen the elect of their dream."

Hennida hid her head in her sister's bosom.

"It would have been better for me not to have seen him, for he doesn't love me."

"He will love you."

"Oh, don't lure me with deceptive hopes. The day when I saw him for the first time, I shivered in sensing that a mysterious amour reigned over his life. And while his image entered into my heart like a sword-thrust, I wept in understanding that another heart than mine inhabited his gaze."

Holwennioul turned the tearful face of the child gently and extended her hand. A beautiful roseate bird flew away into the calm sky.

"Do you see it flying into the heavens, the dove hope?"

And with a wild gesture, she enveloped her sister in her arms, lowering her eyelids over the gulfs of her eyes, perhaps tempestuous for having plunged deep into the entrails of destiny.

Certainly, the dream of embracing a woman like Holwennioul must have burned in the breasts of many men. But who would have dared to hope to trouble the unfathomable ocean of her thought with a frisson? In order for a man not to dread crying amour to her, it was necessary that the vertigo of a passionate youth had disturbed his brain.

Holwennioul was a virgin. Instructed in all the mystery of the temple, her beautiful forehead of a prophetess, a crypt in which knowledge lived, knew all the laws of being. Virginity conserved for her a large part of her strength and her conquering grandeur. The arms of a lover would have absorbed something of her energy, which she was jealously intent on concentrating toward a supreme goal. No assault had corroded the essence of her will in the work of ascension toward the Divine, the impetus of which would have been weighed down by the burden of a terrestrial amour. For the creatures of heroism, for the exceptionally elevated, virginity is a talisman that confirms them in a part of their empire over worlds unknown to the vulgar. Those who give it away abandon a sector of their sphere of action and diminish the radiation of their power.

Was a regret brooding in that woman, in the plenitude of her youth, of never having invited a man to the feast of her beauty? In the time of her efflorescence, among the emotions of spring, had she caressed the dream of leaning her head on the robust shoulder of a beloved individual? Was it without bitterness that she plunged into the solitude from which a soul of light or darkness emerges?

Since she had learned about Hennida's amour, her meditation had darkened. So her fatal beauty had captivated the man that her sister loved!

A theurge, she knew the redoubtable art of manipulating the human passions. But those passions, like all forces, can only be directed, not broken, under the penalty of producing psychic cataclysms. One can deflect a river, but one cannot suppress it.

Loharn, the young man who had fallen at her feet clamoring his adoration for her, whom Hennida had not been able to glimpse unconscious without fainting, was a pastor, twenty years old. A savage adolescent, the air of pure nights and the light of the stars had accumulated candor in his blue eyes, and the custom of living with animals and plants, had nourished his heart with simplicity. To those who exist within her, nature gives a profound and contemplative beauty. A glad mother, because that child loved her, she had adorned him with the charm exhaled from things; and because his soul lived in unison with universal life, she had enriched it with unsuspected grandeurs. He understood the skies and the sea on the edge of which he indulged his juvenile dreams every day. He understood the silence of horizons, which vibrates like the voice of the gods. The soul of things had impregnated his spirit. When such a man is drawn into the orbit of a passion, he circles it under the violent impulsion of his condensed energies. Thus his being, absorbed by the vertigo of amour radiating around Holwennioul, had rushed thereinto like a noble animal chased toward a gulf by the rod of fatality.

On the evening when, in a room hollowed out in the heart of a granite subterrain, he was dazzled to find himself in the presence of Holwennioul, he wondered whether some demonic hallucinator was not toying with an innocent pastor.

In the light of green and roseate torches, the young woman was marching, clad in a bright blue robe fastened with beryls. Above her forehead, amid the night of her hair, shone a five-pointed bronze star.

Certainly, Loharn, in the limbo of his feverish hopes, had not seen the possibility of such a meeting surge forth. As soon as she entered, an anxiety oppressed his breast, before he had even darted a glance at the tragic face of the priestess. For every living being creates in its magnetic respiration, proportionate to its individuality, a sentimental atmosphere, the temporary character of which is immediately discerned by amorous intuition.

"Oh," he cried, carried away by the intoxication of the young woman's approach, "only listen to the voice of my amour; then you will make of my life what you will, for its days are now yours."

Holwennioul turned her pensive head toward him; her smile was sad and soft.

"I know," Loharn continued, "that the folly of loving you leads to death; but all my forces impel me toward you as night impels moths toward the light. And the only happiness I desire is that of entering into sweet death under the auspices of your will."

Holwennioul's gaze gripped the young pastor with the force of an eagle's claw. Accustomed to penetrate the revelation of souls via forms, she measured the juvenile heroism of that face.

"Might you be the strong soul that I hope, young man?"

A blush of joy rushed to the pastor's cheeks. He glimpsed—oh, frail as yet—the hope of being loved.

"Put me to the proof!"

She smiled at that pride.

"Listen: the stars have put over your youth the double seal of amour and death. There are men whose life is prey to amour. You are one of those who cannot renounce their ideal of love. But in loving me one dies of despair. You, I would like to save from the abyss to which you are running. I could give you euthanasia, the blissful death that bears the soul in ecstasy all the way to the bosom of the gods."

"Oh, the supreme dream, to expire under your kiss!"

"Don't hope for that, child. I am one who has never deigned to lie, even to irradiate a lamentable soul with the happiness of illusion. No, my kiss will never brush any man's lips. I belong to the fiancé who awaits me in another world, possessing my impassive fidelity. I am consecrated to divine amour. The beyond of the amour that only twice-born mortals know down here, I can reveal to you the Arcanum; for that fragment of the unique Verity that the ignorance of humans cannot understand, your fine ingenuity will comprehend. Open to that solar radiation your eaglet eye!

"Every being searches instinctively in amour for the door that leads to the androgynic unity. It is necessary to find the complementary being, the heterosexual part of oneself. Some, predestined beings who cross the degrees of evolution more rapidly, cannot encounter the complementary individual on earth. In order to go to melt into the other, under the flame of the first kiss, their virginal soul must await the wings of death. Now, I am one of those. How many times my eyes, of which nature has parted the apparent veils, have contemplated in the nocturnal solitude the certain image of the mysterious fiancé!"

The beautiful narrator paused, lowering her eyelids as if to brush a memory. All that was audible in the silence was the young man's respiration, still labored, but calming down under the oppressive enchantment of Holwennioul's voice.

"Oh," she went on, "why am I wasting time talking about me? I am weary of walking in the cloud of desire woven be men around my beauty."

"Do you not have any pity for those who suffer from having known you?"

"Into the sanctuary of my heart, no one has looked except the gods."

"Oh, imminent death would be dearer to me if I were sure of at least having agitated a frisson of pity."

Slowly, under the tenacious gaze of the young woman, the pastor felt himself invaded by a mental trouble. It seemed a renovation of his soul, bathed as if by lustral water by the projection of those profound pupils.

"If they knew your destiny, it is not with their pity but their envy that men would accompany it. You think you love me! Your novice passion has come to me like a fascinated bird. But I will dissipate the illusion of your amour with a breath. And the virgin of whose love you are unaware, the one who loves you for death, I will deliver to the ecstasy of your arms, liberated from the embrace of an excessively heavy dream. Know the somber beauty of your fate. She will come to you, the one you will recognize as the complement of your being. And when you see her with eyes from which the scales have fallen, all the atoms of yourself will go to her under the effort of an invincible affinity.

"O rare couple, you delight will have for its only issue the fortunate death that will carry you away, reconstituted in a sole and total individuality, toward the ascension of the eternal becoming. Thus commands the Norm. When a man and a woman encounter one another, each being the complement of the other, the shock of the first kiss snatches them from the earth, where they no longer need to live, having recovered the androgynic unity. Procreation, the duty of summoning a new soul to the spiral of involution, belongs to other couples, whose union is less sacred; for the binary must always be resolved by the ternary if it does not revert to the original unity. But how can you, a simple child of the forest, comprehend the mystery of Number, to which the human herd will never accede? You, prepare yourself for the double celebration of amour and death!"

Holwennioul disappeared; the young man remained in the tumultuous isolation of his consciousness. Did the vanishing of that vision tear the young heart of that passionate individual, as if it were ripping away a piece of his flesh? No, the woman's voice had swayed his soul in the waves of its sonorities as the sea once rolled his adolescent muscles. That voice had enveloped him in a network of secret influences. He waited, charmed, for the exitial hour.

Soon, a slight sound made him turn his head. A cry rose to his lips. Holwennioul had returned, holding her sister by the hand. Smaller and frailer, Hennida dazzled the pastor with her radiance. Her long solar hair flowed over a crimson robe tightened at the waist by a belt with a ruby clasp. Around her forehead a circle of gold enlivened the brightness of her chrysophrene pupils, and large golden bracelets, rising at equal intervals from the wrist to the shoulder weighed down the adorable gesture of her right hand, in which a fan made of sparrowhawk plumes was quivering.

At the entrance to the room, Holwennioul, hugging her sister to her breast, had caressed that tender head with a long, very long kiss. The atmosphere of amorous attraction enveloping her splendor, she had been able to detach, by a formidable projection of her will, in order to cloak her sister with it. Thus, Hennida walked in a fluidic ambiance capable of aspiring passion and absorbing desire. Amour went toward her vertiginously, under the irresistible pressure that throws iron toward a magnet, gold toward amphitane and the tail of the mystic serpent toward the hiatus of its mouth. Then again, had she not also, to multiply her charm, faith in her fortunate strength and the certainty of plucking the flower of her dream?

The young man became intoxicated in contemplating the blonde child.

"Is it not the case," Holwennioul said to him, "that you will love her eternally?"

Loharn, with all the energies of his possessed soul, summoned Hennida to the unique fervor of his extended arms.

The gleams of the morning penetrated into the room, the green and pink wall-hangings of which were impregnated by a floating perfume of myrtle and vervain. On crossing the threshold, Holwennioul felt her breast traversed by a heavy frisson, in respiring air through which the funereal angel had passed.

She looked: on the bright blue couch, two bodies were enlaced in the peace of their motionless and very pale beauty. In petrifying their young forms, death had perpetuated the ecstasy of lovers who were still contemplating one another, recklessly, with their wide open eyes, mastered by the frightful fixity of the eyes of cadavers. Gently, Holwennioul closed their eyelids. She knelt down, leaned on the edge of the couch, and, caressing the recumbent couple with her somber eyes, she let her mind wander.

Oh, her beloved sister had quit the earth in the felicity of total amour. A fragile golden flower, since destiny had to pluck her, at least it had taken her with a maternal delicacy. The mysterious art of the priestess had accomplished its work; it had constrained death to be divinely good.

Holwennioul touched the sororal flesh; her hand felt it as cold and hard as granite. She searched that sweet remnant for the vestige of the supreme sentiment that had agitated it; and the inert form revealed infallibly the secret of a triumphal joy. Her slender elegance seemed to be still palpitating with a distant delight, and signified the happy exaltation that did not belie either the model of the widened hips or the proud blossoming of the pointed breasts attesting the vocation of that youth to amour

There was no doubt. The frail child had expired in the ineffable bliss with which desire disquieted her life, a soul borne away by the dove of her ideal into the skies of her hope, fleeing the unhappiness of the base world, the sadness of growing old and the anguish of suffering. Fortunate are those who return, perfumed with youth and ingenuous amour, to the seven times sacred bosom of the gods.

Suddenly, the priestess shivered. A dolorous disturbance whipped her soul. What if her work of euthanasia had wounded the beloved sister? What if the child had wanted to go on living, and enjoying the pleasure of their world and the intoxication of loving?

In order for the possibility of a resurrection to subsist, it was necessary to make haste. Two vital principles having abandoned the gracious body of the dead woman, the liberated soul had not submitted either to time or distance, but, prey to the slow and progressive toil of disincarnation, perhaps the plastic mediator was already dissolving gradually in the circle of sidereal attractions;

and if it were too late, the most imperious command of theurgy would not be able to constrain the corporeal dwelling to reintegrate.

Holwennioul threw a handful of incense into the perfume-burner. She unhooked a sword—the sword, the crucial sign with which virtuality orders the quadruple beam of forces, and whose sharp point maintains the occult fluids.

Holding the sword in her left hand, she seized one of the dead woman's hands in her left, and with an abrupt traction, drew the cadaver toward her lips, appealing to her with a strangely loud clamor:

"Hennida!"

Time went by while the room was still vibrating with that voice accustomed to manipulating the mysterious virtues of sonorities.

The question mentally posed, Holwennioul fixed her intense gaze upon the cherished body, and heard the mute response of a soul descend into the profound silences of her being.

"Don't trouble me any longer; I have my happiness!"

The priestess allowed the charming pale torso to fall back delicately on to the couch, and with a gentle authority, she pronounced:

"Peace be with you, my sister!"

A tear scintillated in her long eyelashes at the contemplation of that beloved form, which would soon be effaced from the visible world by the action of eternal rebirths. She shredded roses over the serenity of the lovers.

And sensing dully within her a melancholy attraction toward death, she stood up, her hand on her breast.

After she had struck a bronze bell with a hammer, a young woman entered, a white silhouette.

"Let the sacred daughters accompany with their incantations and their prayers the flight of two young pure souls!"

Soon, choirs of voices rose up in the gilded morning, a sonorous communion of benevolent wills enveloping the beautiful dead couple in the double nimbus of music and prayer, the two most magisterial of all the forms of the omnipotent Word.

SF & FANTASY

Adolphe Alhaiza. *Cybele*

Alphonse Allais. *The Adventures of Captain Cap*

Henri Allorge. *The Great Cataclysm*

Guy d'Armen. *Doc Ardan: The City of Gold and Lepers; The Troglodytes of Mount Everest/The Giants of Black Lake; The Abominable Snowman*

G.-J. Arnaud. *The Ice Company*

André Arnyvelde. *The Ark; The Mutilated Bacchus*

Charles Asselineau. *The Double Life*

Henri Austruy. *The Eupantophone; The Olotelepan; The Petitpaon Era*

Barillet-Lagargousse. *The Final War*

Barbot de Villeneuve.*The Naiads/Beauty & The Beast*

Cyprien Bérard. *The Vampire Lord Ruthwen*

S. Henry Berthoud. *Martyrs of Science; The Angel Asrael*

Aloysius Bertrand. *Gaspard de la Nuit*

Richard Bessière. *The Gardens of the Apocalypse; The Masters of Silence*

Chevalier de Béthune. *The World of Mercury*

Albert Bleunard. *Ever Smaller*

Félix Bodin. *The Novel of the Future*

Pierre Boitard. *Journey to the Sun*

Louis Boussenard. *Monsieur Synthesis*

Alphonse Brown. *City of Glass; The Conquest of the Air*

Émile Calvet. *In a Thousand Years*

André Caroff. *The Terror of Madame Atomos; Miss Atomos; The Return of Madame Atomos; The Mistake of Madame Atomos; The Monsters of Madame Atomos; The Revenge of Madame Atomos; The Resurrection of Madame Atomos; The Mark of Madame Atomos; The Spheres of Madame Atomos; The Wrath of Madame Atomos* (w/M. & Sylvie Stéphan); *The Sins of Madame Atomos* (w/M. & Sylvie Stéphan)

Jean Carrère. *The End of Atlantis*

Charlotte-Rose Caumont de La Force. *The Land of Delights*

Félicien Champsaur. *Homo-Deus; The Human Arrow; Nora, The Ape-Woman; Ouha, King of the Apes; Pharaoh's Wife*

Didier de Chousy. *Ignis*

Jules Clarétie. *Obsession*

Jacques Collin de Plancy. *Voyage to the Center of the Earth*

Michel Corday. *The Eternal Flame; The Lynx* (w/André Couvreur)
André Couvreur. *Caresco, Superman; The Exploits of Professor Tornada* (3 vols.); *The Necessary Evil*
Gaston Danville. *The Perfume of Lust*
Camille Debans. *The Misfortunes of John Bull*
Captain Danrit. *Undersea Odyssey*
C. I. Defontenay. *Star (Psi Cassiopeia)*
Charles Derennes. *The People of the Pole*
Georges Dodds (anthologist). *The Missing Link*
Charles Dodeman. *The Silent Bomb*
Harry Dickson. *The Heir of Dracula; Harry Dickson vs. The Spider*
Jules Dornay. *Lord Ruthven Begins*
Alfred Driou. *The Adventures of a Parisian Aeronaut*
Odette Dulac. *The War of the Sexes*
Alexandre Dumas. *The Return of Lord Ruthven; The Man who Married a Mermaid* (w/P. Lacroix)
Renée Dunan. *Baal; The Ultimate Pleasure*
J.-C. Dunyach. *The Night Orchid; The Thieves of Silence*
Henri Duvernois. *The Man Who Found Himself*
Achille Eyraud. *Voyage to Venus*
Henri Falk. *The Age of Lead*
Paul Féval. *Anne of the Isles; Knightshade; Revenants; Vampire City; The Vampire Countess; The Wandering Jew's Daughter*
Paul Féval, *fils. Felifax, the Tiger-Man*
Charles de Fieux. *Lamékis*
Fernand Fleuret. *Jim Click*
Charles-Marie Flor O'Squarr. *Phantoms*
Louis Forest. *Someone is Stealing Children in Paris*
Arnould Galopin. *Doctor Omega; Doctor Omega and the Shadowmen* (anthology)
Judith Gautier. *Isoline and the Serpent-Flower*
H. Gayar. *The Marvelous Adventures of Serge Myrandhal on Mars*
Louis Geoffroy. *The Apocryphal Napoleon*
G.L. Gick. *Harry Dickson and the Werewolf of Rutherford Grange*
Raoul Gineste. *The Second Life of Doctor Albin*
Delphine de Girardin. *Balzac's Cane*
Emmanuel Gorlier. *The Nyctalope and the Tower of Babel*
Léon Gozlan. *The Vampire of the Val-de-Grâce*
Jules Gros. *The Fossil Man*
Jimmy Guieu. *The Polarian-Denebian War* (2 vols.)
Edmond Haraucourt. *Daah, the First Human; Illusions of Immortality*

Nathalie Henneberg. *The Green Gods*

Eugène Hennebert. *The Enchanted City*

Jules Hoche. *The Maker of Men and His Formula*

V. Hugo, P. Foucher & P. Meurice. *The Hunchback of Notre-Dame*

Romain d'Huissier. *Hexagon: Dark Matter*

Jules Janin. *The Magnetized Corpse*

Gustave Kahn. *The Tale of Gold and Silence*

Gérard Klein. *The Mote in Time's Eye; Starmasters*

Fernand Kolney. *Love in 5000 Years*

Paul Lacroix. *Danse Macabre; The Man who Married a Mermaid* (w/Alexandre Dumas)

Louis-Guillaume de La Follie. *The Unpretentious Philosopher*

Jean de La Hire. *The Fiery Wheel; Enter the Nyctalope; The Nyctalope on Mars; The Nyctalope vs. Lucifer; The Nyctalope Steps In; Night of the Nyctalope; Return of the Nyctalope; The Nyctalope and the Tower of Babel*

Etienne-Léon de Lamothe-Langon. *The Virgin Vampire The Mysterious Hermit of the Tomb*

André Laurie. *Spiridon*

Gabriel de Lautrec. *The Vengeance of the Oval Portrait*

Alain le Drimeur. *The Future City*

Georges Le Faure & Henri de Graffigny. *The Extraordinary Adventures of a Russian Scientist Across the Solar System* (2 vols.)

Gustave Le Rouge. *The Dominion of the World* (w/G. Guitton) (4 vols.); *The Mysterious Doctor Cornelius* (3 vols.); *The Vampires of Mars*

Jules Lermina. *The Battle of Strasbourg; Mysteryville; Panic in Paris; The Secret of Zippelius; To-Ho and the Gold Destroyers*

Maurice Level. *The Gates of Hell*

M.-J. L'Héritier de Villandon. *The Robe of Sincerity*

André Lichtenberger. *The Centaurs; The Children of the Crab*

Maurice Limat. *Mephista*

Listonai. *The Philosophical Voyager*

Jean-Marc & Randy Lofficier. *Edgar Allan Poe on Mars; The Katrina Protocol; Pacifica 1, 2; Robonocchio; Return of the Nyctalope;* (anthologists) *Tales of the Shadowmen 1-14; The Vampire Almanac* (2 vols.)

Ch. Lomon & P.-B. Gheuzi. *The Last Days of Atlantis*

Charles Malato. *Lost!*

Maurice Magre. *The Marvelous Story of Claire d'Amour; The Call of the Beast; Priscilla of Alexandria; The Angel of Lust; The Mystery of the Tiger; The Poison of Goa; Lucifer; The Blood of Toulouse; The Albigensian Treasure; Jean de Fodoas; Melusine; The Brothers of the Virgin Gold*

Victor Margueritte. *The Bacheloress; The Companion; The Couple*

Camille Mauclair. *The Virgin Orient*

Xavier Mauméjean. *The League of Heroes*

Louis-Sébastien Mercier. *The Iron Man*

Joseph Méry. *The Tower of Destiny*

Hippolyte Mettais. *Paris Before the Deluge; The Year 5865*

Louise Michel. *The Human Microbes; The New World*

Miral-Viger. *The Ring of Light*

Tony Moilin. *Paris in the Year 2000*

Michael Moorcock's *Legends of the Multiverse*

José Moselli. *Illa's End*

John-Antoine Nau. *Enemy Force*

Marie Nizet. *Captain Vampire*

Charles Nodier. *Trilby and The Crumb Fairy*

C. Nodier, A. Beraud & Toussaint-Merle. *Frankenstein*

Oksana & Gil Prou. *Outre-Blanc*

Henri de Parville. *An Inhabitant of the Planet Mars*

Gaston de Pawlowski. *Journey to the Land of the 4th Dimension*

Georges Pellerin. *The World in 2000 Years*

Ernest Pérochon. *The Frenetic People*

Pierre Pelot. *The Child Who Walked on the Sky*

Jean Petithuguenin. *An International Mission to the Moon*

J. Polidori, C. Nodier, E. Scribe. *Lord Ruthven the Vampire*

P.-A. Ponson du Terrail. *The Immortal Woman; The Vampire and the Devil's Son; The Police Agent*

Georges Price. *The Missing Men of the* Sirius

René Pujol. *The Chimerical Quest*

Edgar Quinet. *Ahasuerus; The Enchanter Merlin*

Jean Rameau. *Arrival; in the Stars*

Henri de Régnier. *A Surfeit of Mirrors*

Maurice Renard. *The Blue Peril; Doctor Lerne; The Doctored Man; A Man Among the Microbes; The Master of Light*

Restif de la Bretonne. *The Discovery of the Austral Continent by a Flying Man; Posthumous Correspondence* (3 vols.); *The Fay Ouroucoucou* (2 vols.)

Jean Richepin. *The Crazy Corner; The Wing*

Albert Robida. *The Adventures of Saturnin Farandoul; Chalet in the Sky; The Clock of the Centuries; The Electric Life; The Engineer Von Satanas; In 1965*

J.-H. Rosny Aîné. *Helgvor of the Blue River; The Givreuse Enigma; The Mysterious Force; The Navigators of Space; Pan's Flute; Vamireh; The World of the Variants; The Young Vampire*

Marcel Rouff. *Journey to the Inverted World*

Marie-Anne de Roumier-Robert. *The Voyage of Lord Seaton to the Seven Planets*

Léonie Rouzade. *The World Turned Upside Down*

Han Ryner. *The Human Ant; The Superhumans*

Henri de Saint-Georges. *The Green Eyes*

Louis-Claude de Saint-Martin. *The Crocodile*

X.B. Saintine. *Jonathan the Visionary; The Second Life*

Frank Schildiner. *The Quest of Frankenstein; The Triumph of Frankenstein; Napoleon's Vampire Hunters; The Devil-Plague of Naples*

Nicolas Ségur. *The Human Paradise; Penelope's Secret*

Pierre de Selenes: *An Unknown World*

Norbert Sevestre. *Sâr Dubnotal: Vs. Jack the Ripper; The Astral Trail*

Angelo de Sorr. *The Vampires of London*

Brian Stableford. *The Empire of the Necromancers (1. The Shadow of Frankenstein; 2. Frankenstein and the Vampire Countess; 3. Frankenstein in London); The Wayward Muse; Eurydice's Lament; The Mirror of Dionysius; The Pool of Mnemosyne; The New Faust at the Tragicomique; Sherlock Holmes and The Vampires of Eternity; The Stones of Camelot* (anthologist) *News from the Moon; The Germans on Venus; The Supreme Progress; The World Above the World; Nemoville; Investigations of the Future; The Conqueror of Death; The Revolt of the Machines; The Man With the Blue Face; The Aerial Valley; The New Moon; The Nickel Man; On the Brink of the World's End; The Mirror of Present Events; The Humanisphere*

Jacques Spitz. *The Eye of Purgatory*

Kurt Steiner. *Ortog*

Michel & Sylvie Stéphan. *The Wrath of Madame Atomos* (w/André Caroff); *The Sins of Madame Atomos* (w/André Caroff)

Eugène Thébault. *Radio-Terror*

Edmond Thiaudière. *Singular amours*

C.-F. Tiphaigne de La Roche. *Amilec*

Simon Tyssot de Patot. *The Strange Voyages of Jacques Massé and Pierre de Mésange*

Louis Ulbach. *Prince Bonifacio*

Théo Varlet. *The Castaways of Eros; The Golden Rock.; The Martian Epic* (w/Octave Joncquel); *Timeslip Troopers* (w/André Blandin); *The Xenobiotic Invasion*

Pierre Véron. *The Merchants of Health*

Paul Vibert. *The Mysterious Fluid*

Villiers de l'Isle-Adam. *The Scaffold; The Vampire Soul*

Gaston de Wailly. *The Murderer of the World*

Philippe Ward. *Artahe; Manhattan Ghost* (w/Mickael Laguerre); *The Song of Montségur* (w/Sylvie Miller)